Mothers and Daughters

Also by Vedrana Rudan

Night

Love at Last Sight

Vedrana Rudan

MOTHERS AND DAUGHTERS

A Novel

Translated from Croatian by
Will Firth

DALKEY ARCHIVE PRESS

Originally published in Croatian by
V.B.Z. as *Dabogda te majka rodila* in 2010.

First Dalkey Archive edition, 2018.

Library of Congress Cataloging-in-Publication Data

Names: Rudan, Vedrana, 1949- author. | Firth, Will, translator.
Title: Mothers and daughters / Vedrana Rudan ; translated from the Croatian by Will Firth.
Other titles: Dabogda te majka rodila. English
Description: First Dalkey Archive edition. | McLean, IL : Dalkey Archive Press, 2018.
Identifiers: LCCN 2018026161 | ISBN 9781628972931 (pbk. : acid-free paper)
Classification: LCC PG1620.28.U3 D3313 2018 | DDC 891.8/236—dc23
LC record available at https://lccn.loc.gov/2018026161

www.dalkeyarchive.com
McLean, IL / Dublin

Printed on permanent/durable acid-free paper.

The publication of this book is supported by a grant from the Ministry of Culture of the Republic of Croatia.

The European Commission support for the production of this publication does not constitute an endorsement of the contents which reflects the views only of the author, and the commission cannot be held responsible for any use which may be made of the information contained therein.

For daughters and their moms

1

My husband licked the prawns all over and tipped white wine into his mouth from a tall, slender glass. Garlic was in the air. I sat on the couch, felt my stomach in my throat, and watched the phone. Should I call or wait for her to ring? I was afraid of my mother, I felt guilty despite her being in the best nursing home in Croatia. The home is a large building on a hummock surrounded by a park. Lavender, rosemary, laurel, and banks of flowers. The parking lot in front of the main entrance is almost always full, because children are continually coming to visit their infirm parents. SUVs, Audis, Mercedes, and the occasional expensive Japanese model. When you enter the building you're not hit by the smell of crapped diapers, dirty old skin, urine, and the stench of rotting human beings noisily putrefying. The door of every room has a little sign with the given name and surname of the two men or women in the beds beyond the door. The walls are white, studded with photographs of old people in carnival masks, old people in front of mountain cabins, old people on the waterfront promenade . . . We, who pay, can see right at the entrance that our old mother or father will depart into death happier than happy. The restaurant is on the first floor, separated from the garden by big glass windows; a carafe is in the middle of every table, each with an orange-colored liquid in it. I often passed through the restaurant, at every hour of the day. It was almost always empty and every single time carafes full of orange liquid stood on the tables. The restaurant made a sterile impression, as if no one ever ate even a crust of bread there, although about eighty people lived in the home. I found out that some were my age. I felt uncomfortable when the owner told me that. I really wouldn't want to spend the last years of my life on excursions led by an overly cheerful young woman in a pink coat. I've known the owner for years. The day before my mother was accepted at the home, he and I sat in the enormous auditorium, at a conference table. What kind of conferences were held here? Who sat at such a huge table, what did they speak about, what did they plan . . . I didn't seek an explanation from the owner because I was afraid my mother might lose her place in this institution at the final moment. A documentary was to be made in a few days' time. He poured me a large glass of water: "Did you see the restaurant? We eat there too." "We" meant him and his wife. I smiled at him the way I smile at complete strangers I want to make a good impression on. I sent him a message saying I'd be very glad to entrust my mother to his team. You wait for years for a place in state-run homes. They're much cheaper—you can get a tiny one-room apartment for three or four thousand kuna.

In my city there is also an institution where they put maniacs, geriatrics, underage lesbians, and underage gays, whose parents think a stay among maniacs and geriatrics will set their children back on track. The accommodation is cheap there too, but the manager knows me and said to me in confidence: "Perhaps this shouldn't be the first choice for your mother. Before you bring her here from the hospital it might be good to have a look yourself and see what it's like. You know, there's a shortage of staff and a lot of patients, and even the four-bed rooms are all taken up. If you really intend to come, please be prepared for what you're going to see."

I backed out.

Two streets from our house is a small old people's home with just a few rooms. That appealed to me most because my mother would be close by, but still far enough away. I'd be able to visit her every day, or several times a day, and then leave her room and shut her out of my head until the next day. I called the owner of the small home.

"What condition is your mother in?" he asked.

"Normal, I suppose," I said.

"Is she independent and mobile?"

"She could be mobile, but for the time being she refuses to walk or eat at the table."

"So she's not in a terminal phase?"

"No, far from that, she's going to outlive you and me." I wanted to cheer up the doctor and tell him my mom wouldn't cause much work.

"Good, come and have a look, I'm sure we'll reach an agreement. The price is three thousand five hundred kuna a month, comprehensive care."

"What does that include?"

"Everything."

The home was a one-story yellow building located between the fish market called Tuna and Tomo's Butchers. A dark-blue, iron tuna dangled above the door of the fish market. From the front of the shop where meat was sold, big ox eyes watched me sadly from an ox head without a body. Next to Tomo's was a dental surgeon. The stomatologist greeted his patients with a giant molar. A threat? A promise? It was a good thing that I walked there, otherwise I wouldn't have found anywhere to park. I rang. The doctor himself opened the door for me. He had donned a white coat over his suit; it was unbuttoned, he had a light-blue shirt, a dark-red tie, black shoes, and he watched me with his blue eyes. Around his neck, a stethoscope. Why do doctors always wear a stethoscope around their necks, even when they're in their little office talking with patients' relatives? A doctor, a real doctor, always has to be prepared—what if the relatives suddenly felt sick when they heard how much they'd be paying for grandmother's heart scan?

"You're well?" the gentleman in the dark suit asked after closing the door behind me.

"Yes, thanks," I smiled bravely. I always smile when I feel uncomfortable, and I certainly felt it now—discomfort and a jolt from the overpowering stench of urine and feces.

"You're pale," the doctor said. "Shall I show you the room or do you feel our institution isn't what you expected?"

"Show me the room." My stomach squirmed in my throat.

He opened the door of a dark room of about ten by twenty feet. Eight beds. Grotesque contorted figures covered by sheets. Fluid was flowing into some of them, others stared rigidly at the ceiling. The stench was unbearable. I looked at the doctor, I wanted him to move, he was in my way, but he stood there in the doorway and didn't budge.

"It's hard to find carers these days, unfortunately. No one wants to work, and everyone complains."

Something began to howl in the corner next to the window.

"Old Ana's been restless recently."

I pushed him aside, Armani penetrated my nose, I rushed for the door and grabbed hold of the handle, but it was locked.

The doctor touched me on the back. "Please, come and sit down for a moment."

Trembling, I dropped into a comfortable red armchair.

The doctor sat down next to me and placed his well-manicured hand on mine, which was well manicured and shaking. "Calm down, it's all right . . ."

"That's terrible, terrible, Jesus, I think I'm going to be sick . . ."

"No, you're not. Just breathe, breathe."

I breathed and breathed, and his blue eyes smiled at me.

"Death is abhorrent if you see it as something nasty, something that only happens to the bad and to others. You shouldn't let such prejudices get the better of you."

"But the people should be washed . . ."

"We do wash them, but we don't get around to it often enough, the carers keep resigning on us."

"I know death is normal and we all have to die someday . . . ," I began to cry, why, I don't know, "but like this . . ."

"You know . . ." The doctor glanced at his cell phone and rejected the call. "Just alter your point of view. Imagine this room where the old people are now as one full of babies in diapers, and everything will seem different. It's strange that people think old folks' shit stinks, but when it comes to baby doo-doo in diapers they even find it cute, as long as it's not diarrhea. Why the difference? All of us shit and piss, and we all stink. These folks here don't know what's happening to them, they're not suffering. There are a million ways to kill pain these days. They're waiting for their final hour, and it's all painless. It's a great achievement for people to die without pain."

"Yes, it's a great achievement." I heaved myself out of the armchair. "Could you please open the door for me? My mom wouldn't be happy here."

"I respect your choice, madam." He offered me his hand.

I looked at the door. If I accepted his hand he'd open it, if I refused he'd plunge a needle into me, and then who knows how long I'd have to perish there painlessly in the reek of shit and piss. I gripped his hand firmly and gave a hearty laugh: "If I'd known about you I would have brought my father here, unfortunately it's too late for that now."

"Think about what I told you. For old people, the most important thing is that they're not in pain. Homes are excessively expensive today, everyone wants to make money on the weak and frail. Our price is more than fair."

I went out into the glaring morning light. Buses and trucks thundered along the broad street. I needed something to drink, something strong, that instant. A song resounded in the Vijolica tavern. Drunken male voices were singing "a bunch of flowers that comes from the hills" in Italian—*quel mazzolin di fiori che vien dalla montagna* . . . I changed my mind and wanted to go straight home. But then I looked at the ox head on the front of the shop, and when I turned my gaze I saw the big molar. I puked my guts out on the crosswalk. A young mom was pushing a stroller. The little girl smiled at me. I ran to the other side so as not to end up under the wheels of a bus. My mom had to have the best, only the best was good enough for my mom, even if it cost nine thousand kuna we'd pay nine thousand kuna. My mom would never become a thing waiting in its own shit until God finally had mercy. Never!

"I'm glad your carer ladies are constantly smiling," I said to my friend, the owner of the Felicita home. He gave me a hearty smile, from ear to ear, as if we hadn't known each other for years, as if I was just another customer. There was no spark in his brown eyes, his teeth were much better than when we last saw each other, when he was running a restaurant in town. "I tell everyone at the very start: 'Sweetheart, if you can't keep up a smile from the beginning to the end of your shift, you needn't apply.' That's why they're cheerful. Just between us, the mother of the richest woman in Croatia lives here. She was here yesterday—the richest woman in Croatia—and she said to me: 'When I grow old, I'm coming here too.'"

I laughed loudly and cheerfully like the female TV-show host chortles at a joke from her male colleague when they present the "Croatian Golden Oldies" together. My mother was supposed to go to the home on the recommendation of the doctor, it wasn't my idea. I never told her it was a home, I'd just mention the term "rehabilitation center" from time to time. She arrived there from the hospital where she'd been after a stroke. They wouldn't have admitted her at the hospital if the head of the department wasn't a good friend of ours. When Tiny found her grandma lying piss-soaked by her bedside, she called an ambulance. "A stroke," the ER doctor said and left again.

We'd been to Vienna, we travel a lot. I called Tiny, and she told me. My husband phoned our neurologist friend, and the next day we met up with him.

"I don't know, I have no idea. She might hang on, or she might exit, you never know. For now, she's alive."

My mother lay in a hospital room strapped to the bed with leather belts. A fat needle was in her neck and fluid dripped into the vein. On the bed next to my mother's lay a young woman. Her husband was calling her name in despair. I knew he was her husband because only spouses and immediate relatives were allowed to visit. He stroked her hand and caressed her face. The woman breathed with a rattle.

"Mom!" I said loudly, because at times my mother would go totally deaf. "How are you?"

She looked at me with bleary eyes.

"How are you?" I raised my tone.

The young man was speaking to his wife: "You have to try and hold on, you can't leave me. Wake up, darling!" He flinched when I yelled at my mother.

"Sorry," I said, not looking at him but at my mother's bound arms, "my mom's deaf."

He didn't reply. I turned toward him and saw his face was wet with tears. A rattle came from his wife's chest.

My mother didn't recognize me. Or she did but was unable to speak. I left feeling shaken up and strangely unprepared. My mother had been in a particularly foul mood recently. She was always complaining about intolerable pain in her back. We took her to the pain clinic and they prescribed her morphium patches. We stuck them on her sore back. One lady looked after her by day, Tiny was with her at night, and everything was under control. But then, overnight, a stroke. And now those leather belts that prevented the spindly body from rolling out of bed and crashing to the floor. So naked and gaunt, she looked like a wizened old Jesus with a greasy perm on his head.

"We'll fill her with fresh blood and give her a few intravenous drips. That will boost her. But you do realize that it's nothing long-term, your mother is already at a ripe old age . . ." Our friend eyed me with concern, as if my mother's life mattered to him and he was worried how I'd take all this. He put his hand on my shoulder and accompanied me to the exit. Ten days later my mother was a new woman.

"I didn't want to tell you," she looked at my husband and me with her pale-brown, watercolor eyes, "but when I felt the leather belts on my arms I thought they'd put me away for not paying my TV subscription. You remember they sentenced me to jail or three days of work for the public good? So I thought this was it . . ."

I was glad my mother was herself again. She really had been sentenced to three days of unpaid community work. Once she carelessly opened her door for two men. They told her they had discovered by X-ray radar that she hadn't been paying her TV subscription, and it would be best for her if she admitted her guilt immediately, because otherwise they'd have to arrest her. So she admitted and signed. She begged us not to protest about the sentence, but we found the whole thing ludicrous. How could anyone take a virtually immobile old woman and force her to do unpaid community work? It was a nightmare for her. For a while, she was so terrified that she barely let me into the apartment. She'd only open the door when my weird howling got through to her periodically stone-deaf ears.

"Mom, you had a stroke because you didn't drink enough fluids and because you overdosed on Ultram. On top of the morphium patches, you were also taking Ultram. You'll have to stop that if you intend to live a bit longer."

"They don't give me anything here to stop the pain, tell them to give me a patch, call them, they have to give me a patch straightaway," she shouted.

I recoiled and glanced at the bed where yesterday the young woman had been. Now an old man was lying there, stark naked and unconscious.

"Don't yell, Mom, there are seriously ill people here. I'll tell them to come and put on a patch."

"When?"

"Right away, I'm going to see the doctor now, hang in there, Mom, I'm going now, because the visits are just fifteen minutes."

"Please tell them I need a patch."

"Morphium patches?! We have her under constant observation, she isn't in pain at all," our friend said.

"But they told us at the pain clinic . . ."

Our friend sneered. "Your mom's simply hooked. She's been here for three weeks and we've taken her off everything, my nurses tell me she's not getting anything at all now. I'm convinced of it too. She breathes calmly when she thinks no one's looking, but as soon as she sees one of us she gets restless. From today on she's off morphium, Ultram, and tranquilizers. And, of course, I'm sure you realize, she needs care twenty-four hours a day. She'll have to go into a home."

"A home?!" I was taken aback.

"Yes, a home. She needs care day and night."

"She has a woman who looks after her."

Our friend became impatient, pulled a cigarette out of its pack, and probed me with his light-brown eyes. The ward my mother had been admitted to was incredibly tidy, with new beds, new blankets, quiet and friendly nurses, and new equipment.

"Donations . . ." He returned the cigarette to the pack. "Without donations this would be a dismal hole."

"She doesn't want to go into a home, she's always said that."

"You don't have to tell her she's going to a home, I'll tell her we're taking her to a rehabilitation center—that sounds nicer. And, by all means, you can add that you'll take her back home when she's better."

"Will she get better?"

"I don't know. At the moment she's well and, most importantly, completely 'clean.' Take no notice of her wailing, she's a manipulator."

The head nurse in the home wore a dark-blue coat. She gave me a big smile. "It doesn't have to be straightaway, but please do tell her as soon as possible that she's in a home. Your mother isn't stupid, and it's better if she hears it from you, rather than the cleaning lady."

"I can't. As long as I can remember, she's said she doesn't want to die in a home. I feel guilty."

"Guilty? The old people here are happy. Have you seen the photographs on the walls? They even have a dance course, they can make lovely paper animals, which helps them develop their motor skills again, we have an entertainer, a hairdresser, a masseur . . . This isn't an almshouse, it's a five-star hotel."

"You know, my mom has grown used to morphium patches. We used to stick them on her back because she had terrible pain, she told us the pain in her back was hideous. When she had the stroke we took her to the hospital, and there they discovered she wasn't in pain at all, my mom was just hooked. They took her off morphine patches, and at the moment she's clean. If she cries and howls and asks for some drug . . ."

The head nurse gave me another big smile. She had blue eyes. "We got the discharge report, don't you worry, we know how to deal with that. They're all the same, always asking for a tranquilizer or something. We'll stick a placebo patch on her back every three days. We don't like to zonk out people here, we like them to be alert. We love them but, as you know, they're like children. Don't you worry, we'll keep her calm without the drugs."

I left the building where my mom was, somewhere. I didn't have the courage to go and see her. I decided I'd visit her in the late afternoon. Visits were allowed the whole day, and if I went at the end of the day, the night would be shorter for her. The nurse told me that the old people have a phone with a direct line on their night tables, there's a TV in the room and a large bathroom, and they eat or are fed five times a day. The women who look after them are constantly smiling, those are the ones with the pink coats. The therapists wear white coats, and the nurses blue ones.

I picked up the receiver.

"Why weren't you up here when they brought me?" she snarled.

"They told me to come once you'd settled in and got used to things a bit. I'll come later, do you need anything?"

"The trip in the ambulance was horrific. Every bone hurt—and still hurts . . ."

"How do you find it up there? It's one of the best rehabilitation centers in Croatia, you have a TV in the room, and a large bathroom. Have you been to the bathroom, have you done a number two today?"

A sneer forced its way through the receiver to my ear: "My daughter, I can't move, I'm hardly alive. If you'd come and see me you'd know what state I'm in. They put me in a diaper . . ."

"Mom, try to perk up a bit and get yourself out of diapers, you're not in intensive care anymore, there's no need to depend on the help of others. And you have to exercise every morning, you have to go for a walk, the more the better. A nurse said: 'Your mom has to walk and walk.' And when you've recovered completely, you can come home again . . ."

"Bring me peach-flavor iced tea, tissues, napkins, and baby lotion. They'll give me a rub down with it every day."

"You seem tired somehow. Why are you so lethargic? Thank God the worst is behind you."

"What was the worst?"

"The stroke. You were tied to the bed with leather belts, do you remember? They fed you intravenously . . ."

"When are you going to come?"

"Rabby is sad without you, she keeps gnawing at the grill of the cage. I bought her fresh food, I stroked her on the back a bit, you can really feel how much she misses you, she sniffs the air . . ."

"When are you going to come?"

"Your Italian pension came this morning, brought by a new mailman. He said to me: 'What a wonderful little buck you have, as orange as a brick.' And I told him: 'It's not a buck, it's a doe—a she.'"

"When are you going to come?"

"I thought you might be overtired today and could use a bit of rest. I'll come tomorrow."

She hung up.

2

My father, my dead father, smells of garlic and white wine. I asked my girlfriends, and all of them remember the smell of their father, but not one of them knows how their mother smells. When you google "smell of my mother" in Croatian you get one thousand six hundred hits, but for "smell of my father" Google asks you, "Did you mean 'hello, my father'?" I know how my father smelled, I still have him in my nose today. How does my mother smell? Before she had the stroke, she was in the gastro ward. There, too, the head is a friend of ours. We didn't call an ambulance, I took the pale, almost white, haggard body into the building myself. I carried her, body to body, nose to nose, but in vain. Maybe because she'd been looked after by the lady who used to wash her from head to foot every day.

"I'm dying," she moaned as I lugged her up the front steps. "This is it."

"Don't exaggerate," I groaned. "One doesn't die quite so easily."

I let her slide down off my back. She screamed, so I took hold of her again. I wanted her to be quiet, I couldn't carry her and talk to her at the same time. I hauled my half-dead mother into the hospital and handed her to the doctors. Most of them had gone to school with me, so they paid her a lot of attention. I've lost count of all the tests they did, the scans, blood tests, CTs, colonoscopies . . . Probably I've forgotten something.

"Nothing wrong," the head of the department said to me. "She's healthy, just a bit anemic. We'll give her some fresh blood and she'll be as good as new, but don't expect too much."

"What do you mean?"

"Your mother is over eighty. Those are nice years, when the body slows down although it's still healthy. But my guess is that she's depressive, and I don't know how to get her over that. Find some way of entertaining her, she shouldn't be left alone, find a day carer."

"We have someone."

"Excellent. Your mother really needs professional assistance: feeding several times a day, help with dressing, regular bathing, massage, exercise—that's all too much. We're not young anymore either."

"Yes," I said, "it's all too much for me."

The doctors sent my mother back infused with blood. Although she lived close by, I didn't visit her very often. Whenever I stood at her bedside, the resentful old woman would cover herself up to the neck and watch me with a pale-brown eye. A small pot of black coffee, a pot of tea, and a mass of medicines were on the nightstand, but not Ultram.

"It hurts so bad, but nobody believes me," she'd say.

"We all believe you, and the lady believes you. Look how clean everything is around you, we all take care of you, everyone in their own way, we all love you," I hoped she wouldn't sense the vast impatience and tedium in my voice.

"You don't understand," she snarled, "nobody understands, the pain is unbearable, give me drops."

"The doctor said you mustn't overdo it, you'll get hooked on Ultram . . ."

"Hooked? What are you talking about?"

A week earlier, I found a bottle of Ultram under the sink among the detergents.

"You'll overdose again and fall out of bed. You didn't even wash until the lady came to the house."

"Why didn't you wash me?"

"Because I don't know how to wash grown adults."

"You find me revolting."

"No, I don't find you revolting, but only a qualified person can wash an adult, knows how to move you, hold you, soap you up, without you falling over . . ."

"You find me revolting."

"I don't find you revolting, but when we can afford you the best service there is?"

"It's best when a daughter loves her mother, washes her mother, visits her mother, and listens to what her mother says. I'm in pain, that's why I don't like to wash. Give me Ultram, this pain is killing me . . ."

I dropped six drops into her tea.

"Don't be heartless."

And three more.

"Don't be mean."

And seven more.

She poured the tea down her throat, out of her mind with fear that I might take it away from her. I covered her up and left the apartment. Now I'd killed her. They'd do an autopsy. Would I go to jail? Is it a crime to kill a mother who doesn't want to live? Does she not want to live at all, or not want to live without Ultram? What kind of life is in store for my mother if I don't kill her soon? In the tiny garden in front of my mother's building a dirty-white Maltese dog—whether it was a he or a she didn't matter—spread its hind legs and laid a turd in the gladioli. I'm crazy about flowers. I glanced around, a lady was sticking her head in the dumpster, the coast was clear, so I gave him or her a gentle kick. There are too many dogs in this country.

"Why is no one here?"

"Mom, do you know what time it is?"

"No idea."

"It's five in the morning. Sleep a bit more . . ."

"Sleep, sleep, sleep, I couldn't get a wink of sleep all night. When's someone going to come?"

"I'll come this evening."

"Do you have the car?"

"I do."

"Don't get into the car, do you hear me? You can't drive, you've never been a good driver, I don't want to have you on my conscience."

"All right, I'll take a taxi then."

"You can take the money from my pension, I don't need anything anyway. Ow, it hurts so bad, so bad, so bad, my daughter. Oh, how it hurts."

I hung up in disgust. How long would I have to listen to that nervous, trembling, savage old voice for? And how could I gratify her?

3

It was all Souls' Day, or, to be exact, the day before All Souls' Day. I stood beside his grave, where perhaps his legs were, or what was left of them, and looked at the gravestone. Should I tape over the photograph? My father had himself photographed on his grave, lying on the marble slab and laughing at the photographer. I really need to tape over that photo. My father loved people to consider him a joker. And they did. And still, what would these people, whose opinions my father always thought very highly of, say if they saw a photo of the old man reclining on his gravestone and laughing? People? Who are the people that meant so much to my father when I was fifteen, when I wanted with all my heart to stand on top of my father's grave and cry tears of joy? It seemed to me back then that if you wished hard enough . . . But Coelho hadn't written any of his hit novels yet. I really, truly wished for my father to be struck by lightning, to be eaten by a shark, to fall off the boat into the pitch-black sea while fishing at night, to slip off the ladder and crash onto the concrete while pruning a cypress during the day, to choke on one of the little squid he used to toss ungutted onto the stove burner and then stick down his gullet almost raw, to suffocate when his plastic teeth got stuck in his throat one night, to get bitten by Nika the dog, whom he loved, but she didn't love him . . . None of that happened.

She was lying there with a pink blanket over her. I put the coffee from the vending machine on her nightstand.

"How was she last night?"

The lady who covered up her diapers when I came in and uncovered them again when she saw I was by myself answered angrily: "She was dead to the world all night, but during the day she kept pestering the nurses and asking for painkillers, so they switched off her buzzer. I don't understand. Look at me, see these two legs, I can't feel them, touch here . . ."

I touched the calf of her left leg.

"You see, I don't feel anything, my legs are like two posts, I'm immobile. If I had half the health of your mom I'd be running and jumping about, I wouldn't be here, I'd be at home if I wasn't bedridden . . ."

"What's the lady saying? Is she saying again that I'm not in pain?"

"You're awake!"

"I wasn't asleep, I just had my eyes closed."

"Have you done your exercises today? You have to walk a lot, you have to go to the restaurant every day, you should eat on your own and get rid of the diapers . . ."

"A lady came and photographed me."

"Which lady?"

"One who works here. She said I'm a beautiful old woman. And good-hearted. Her husband said I'm a beautiful old woman, too."

She looked at me. Her short, gray hair had been carelessly cropped and the skull showed through the wisps, she had a large, meaty nose, splotchy skin, one eye closed, dark-red eyelids, a toothless mouth, and inflamed gums.

"Mom, you are beautiful, but you'd be even more beautiful if you put on your glasses, put in your teeth, let the hairdresser curl your hair . . ."

"Everything hurts, every bone in my body, they switched off my buzzer."

"Because you're not patient."

"That lady thinks I'm a good old woman. Did you bring the peach iced tea for me?"

"I forgot, I'll bring it for you tomorrow."

"Who else is coming?"

"Mom, we've arranged to take turns: I'll come one time, Tiny the next, and my husband will come as well."

She closed her eyes. "Pull down my blanket, cover up my feet."

"I'm going. Drink the coffee while it's hot."

"I haven't got a straw."

"Here, the lady will give you hers."

She didn't move. I left the room. At the reception desk there was a lady with Alzheimer's, who waved to me cheerfully, and two men who seemed to be about my age. The receptionist greeted me with a smile from ear to ear. In the meantime someone had stolen my umbrella. The men, Ms. Alzheimer, or the receptionist? I left. A woman in jeans was hosing the lavender and rosemary.

4

When I was small, I wished my father dead, just like I now wish for a day without pain or the fear of death. The newspaper articles that celebrate the extension of people's life span annoy me to no end. Female babies born this year will live to be ninety, male babies eighty. But even today everyone reaches eighty. The articles don't mention how much an eighty-year-plus baby costs. Fortunately, I have the dough, so keeping her alive hasn't killed me financially. I trade in angels. Why angels, of all things? Where did that idea come from? I'll tell you that later. In any case, they're made in Ana's woodworking shop. We grew up together, Ana and I, we gave birth together, she had Jerry and I had Tiny. Jerry's father, Stanko, inherited the workshop from his Grandfather Dušan. As a girl, I used to play in the late Grandfather Dušan's workshop. Whenever I smell sawdust in the air, I remember the coffins that old Grandfather Dušan made. The workshop was enormous, I remember the rafters I used to see from out of the coffin. When Grandfather Dušan died, they put him in a coffin that the late Stanko made for him. Yes, Stanko died too, although he was the same age as me. A healthy man, I never saw him drink or smoke, and spent his life in the sawdust. Ana told me Stanko had hands of gold. Whatever somebody thought up, he'd make it. A wooden toy, a wooden dress, wooden pants, a wooden hat, a wooden spiderweb. He had hands of gold and also used them to make a wooden go-kart. He loved carnival more than anything else in the world. Once a year, the wide road leading from the highway down to my old hometown would be closed off. That day, grown men would race down the hill in wooden go-karts. Whoever crossed the finish line first down at the waterfront promenade was presented a laurel wreath by a young woman dressed up as a harlot. The late Stanko started off downhill in his go-kart, and a Russian who had bought the most beautiful villa in town—before the war it belonged to the Republic of Croatia—set off at full speed uphill. The Russian hasn't fit into life in my native town to this day. Stanko died on the scene of the accident. Little Jerry laid him in a coffin.

I put a piece of tissue in my mouth and called her. The phone rang for a long time. I gave up and tried again an hour later. This time she answered.

"Mom," I muttered with my mouth full of paper.

"Who is it?" her voice trembled.

"It's me," the paper was growing in my mouth.

"Who is it?"

I took the paper out of my mouth. "It's me," I said a bit more articulately.

"What's wrong with you, why are you talking like that?"

"I had a dental operation. They had to cut into my jaw. I'll come early this evening . . ."

"No, don't bother. Take care of yourself," her voice was calm, weak, and concerned.

"Good, see you tomorrow then," I mumbled and hung up.

Yes!

I took three little helpers and fell asleep. I saw the sea from my childhood. I went down the road to the square, I wanted to have a coffee at the Bar if my father wasn't there. He was. An old man, a fisherman, dark glasses on his pale, wrinkled face. Wide fisherman's pants and a flannel shirt, clean (who did his washing?). Did he recognize me? I walked past him the way I normally walked past my father. As if he wasn't there. I was woken by the ringing of my cell phone. Her again?

5

I WANTED TO kill my mother. To get rid of her.

"I want my mom dead, I want my mom dead," I paced around the living room and watched my phone. "I want you dead, dead, dead!"

"Ana says to say hello."

She looked at me dully.

"Ana says to say hello," I yelled, competing with the TV.

"Thanks," she replied. "Today I walked, I was up on the next floor, I took a pee in the toilet, I'm not wearing diapers anymore, my back hurts badly."

"That's not true," the Immobile Lady chimed in. "She's lying, she always lies to you, don't believe anything she says, she took a poop in bed."

"Is she saying bad things about me again?"

"No, the lady said her legs are like two posts."

6

I DIDN'T WANT to put my mother in a home. I told her a hundred times: "Mom, I'll never stick you in a home, never ever."

"Don't expect me to believe that," she'd say, "I know you too well. You're practical—when I become sick and weak you'll get rid of me."

"Why?"

"Because you don't love me. You'll put up with me as long as I can make my own soup, and as soon as I'm decrepit you'll stick me in a home. But I'm telling you: before you take me away to a home, kill me. You know I can't stand having strangers around me."

Whenever we talked about a home, it was always me who broached the subject, and my mother would cry. She'd wipe her nose in a big handkerchief. She refused tissues.

"Mom, there are homes where you can have your own one-room apartment . . ."

"There you go again, what did I tell you," my mother would say.

"Mom, when you're sick and weak we'll find somebody."

"What do you mean 'somebody'?!" It was inconceivable for my mother that an unfamiliar person could come into her life.

"A woman. A lady. A kind-hearted lady."

I didn't know back then what I know today: in Croatia it's impossible to find a day carer to look after one's mother for any length of time. I don't know how many women I talked with. All of them were out of work, and all of them cursed Croatia, where it was impossible to find a job. Their children were out of work, their husbands were out of work, their brothers and sisters were out of work . . .

"I'd like you to shower my mother once a week, you don't need to wash her hair, I'll call her hairdresser. Come at around nine in the morning, make her coffee, during the day she drinks little bottles of iced tea. For lunch, say at about one, she just eats a little rice pudding, that's all. From time to time you should vacuum the apartment, wash the windows when necessary, keep the bathroom clean, change her, put the dishes in the machine, trickle five drops of Ultram in her tea at one thirty, and you're free at two. You don't need to come on weekends. I'm offering three hundred euros, that's what her Italian and Croatian pensions come to."

No woman in Croatia is prepared to work for twenty-four kuna an hour, even though tens of thousands are dying of hunger. We were lucky. We found one who worked for twenty kuna an hour. The ones who came after her were more expensive, thirty-five kuna an hour. Today, I think it was maybe not the price that was the problem as much as them finding it unforgivably arrogant that I refused to take care of my own mother.

"Why should we look after your mother, you lazy cow?" their formless hair, cheap bags, and discount-mart shoes seemed to ask me. I felt uncomfortable when their eyes stabbed into mine, and I considered myself lazy, as well as a hard-hearted, mean, ungrateful bitch, but it was still easier for me to put up with the looks of those women than to wash my mother. What is a child's love for its mother? How long does it last? Were my mother and I actually mother and child, or just two tired old women who both ought to have a right to peace? Why should I have to call her three times a day? If I didn't call her, she'd call me, either on the landline or my cell phone. I didn't go to her apartment so I wouldn't have to see her. While the first "lady" was with her, my mother was clean and fresh, well-fed, and rubbed with every ointment and salve on the market at the time. Horse Balm soothes pain, Tiger Balm cools the skin . . . I couldn't, I really couldn't stand it when her number appeared on the display of the landline at home, or on my cell. I don't understand the world I live in, a world where people only talk over the phone instead of talking in silence. Why is there so much noise, all this ringing? I cower at every sound. Cell phones. I'm surrounded by young parents who don't have the money to pay their electricity and water bills, but their children are constantly getting new phones. So they don't get bullied when they enter the classroom. So the other children don't find out that their parents are homeless suckers and slaves. But that's what the parents are to their children. Why couldn't their child be the first to go into the classroom and say, "I haven't got a cell phone because my folks can't afford one"? Now wouldn't that be heroic? Maybe the first Croatian kid brought up by his parents to be that brave would become a white Obama. I could talk with myself for hours about Obama; finally, we have a black man on the screen who doesn't rap or tap dance, doesn't play soccer or basketball except recreationally, hallelujah! a black man who isn't just his legs or his voice. Who knows how long the Americans will let him go unassassinated? How will they do it? A poisoned candy, a sniper, one of the trendy fevers?

Her voice sounded youthful. "I was good today. I did a number two in the toilet and went for a walk and drank three big cups of milk . . ."

"Mom, don't drink milk, drink tea! Milk is poison. American doctors gave one group of rats pure poison, and another group milk:

the group that ate the poison lived longer. Don't drink milk, don't eat cheese, don't touch yogurt—everything you hear about milk and milk products is propaganda from the manufacturers . . ."

"Speak louder, I can't hear you . . ."

"What I'm trying to say, Mom . . . can you hear me?" I yelled.

"I can hear you."

"Don't drink milk, don't eat cheese, don't touch yogurt. Milk is poison, milk is poison, remember that, milk is poison, American doctors gave one group of rats pure poison, and the other group milk . . ."

"Who believes doctors these days? They're propagandists. If the stories about the nutritional value of milk are propaganda by the dairy farmers, how do you know that the stories about healthy diets with fruit and vegetables aren't propaganda by the fruit and vegetable producers? You've always been naive, obsessive, and hotheaded, you've always believed anything that's well written."

She didn't say this now, but that was the way she talked with me before her illness. Instead, I heard in the receiver: "Why are you yelling? You'd believe anything, but you don't believe me, and I'm in pain, it was unbearable today, it started on the left side of my neck . . ."

"Mom, I have to go and see the eye doctor, he said I'm going blind in my left eye, retinal macular degeneration . . ."

"Speak up a bit . . ."

"The eye doctor told me to come and see him today, I'm going blind in my left eye . . ."

The veins on my neck were as thick as the ropes they use to tie the *Marco Polo* ferry to the waterfront. Or *used* to tie, rather—the ferry's since been scrapped.

"What did you say?"

"Mom, I'm going blind, I'm going blind!"

"Don't yell. What are you behind?"

7

OBAMA WAVED TO us from the screen. It was hot in the room. The Immobile Lady was asleep.

So many people are happy about the advent of Obama. If my father was alive, he would have found it ridiculous. He never believed the stories we were all supposed to believe. He thought President Tito was an old toad. While my sister and I stood spruced up by the roadside and waved little paper flags, he'd stand beside us in his dirtiest gardening pants and a ragged tank top and wave at Tito with a filthy rag. He'd come running up at the last minute and we'd always see him too late. One of my father's friends occasionally worked as a waiter on the Brionian Islands, where Tito had his summer residence, and my sister and I would listen when he told us that Jovanka, Tito's wife, was unable to choose the right dessert; iced coffee can't be served to a hundred people all at once, some got a ball of ice cream on their coffee, but most just had their coffee splotched with ice-cold liquid. My father enjoyed that story. He'd laugh, showing the few gold teeth in his mouth, and he'd let his dark-red eyelids down over his pale-blue eyes as he slapped his hands on his knees. He considered Tito, Jovanka, and the rest of the crew to be freaks who marketed themselves as superiors in a country where everyone was equal. Why am I thinking about my late father? Why can't I stroke my mother's hand?

She sat on the bed dressed in white pajamas. Tiny and I had thrown all her old rags in the garbage. I bought her a mass of new clothes for the home: tank tops, pajamas, little socks in all colors, and two light dressing gowns, yellow and red. I put a red straw in her cup of coffee and raised it to her lips. She refused.

"I'll drink it when you've gone. I only trust him," she pointed at Obama.

"Can you see without your glasses?"

"Because the blacks know what suffering is. If Obama was head of this 'rehabilitation center'—," I felt she glanced at me derisively, or maybe I just imagined it, "he'd give me Ultram. If your father was alive he wouldn't believe Obama. He'd ridicule him: 'Obama, the president who'll give the dirty, sick, gap-toothed blacks their faith in justice back. Obama, the voice of the disenfranchised. Obama, one of us, who carries our cross on his lean, athletic, dark body. Obama, finally a black in these black times, when things are looking black for all blacks, whatever color they may be. Obama Jesus. Obama Savior. Obama Hope. Obama Solution. Obama Light. Obama Joy.'"

She looked at me and grinned like my late father, her face was pink and her faint mustache bedewed.

"You're better, Mom, you're much, much better, you're back to your old self."

She slid deeper into the bed and pulled the blanket up over her head. She was right. If my father was alive, as soon as he heard "Obama" he would have demonstratively reached for his balls in his dirty pants and bared his gold teeth as if to say, "Fuck you!" Later he had the golden veneers taken out, a denture put in, and covered his eyes with dark glasses. If my father was alive and if he had talked with me while he was alive, he would have asked me how I can believe in the good intentions of a man who had two billion dollars pumped into his campaign. If my father was alive, he would have said Obama was a chocolate marionette on the strings of white capitalism. If my father was alive, he would have said Obama was a ruse to blind the gullible, who are forever in search of hope because only delusions can stop a man from shooting himself. If my father was alive, I would have quarreled with him because I thought Tito to be a great man. But my father is dead, and I resemble him more and more. If he rose from the grave, our conversation would be that of two people who see eye to eye. Huh, if someone had told me twenty years ago that I'd agree with my father . . .

"Mom, when you make it to one hundred we'll write to Obama and ask him to send you a card."

"I'd rather they send me Ultram."

8

When did I first think that only a dead father is a good father? Sometime around when I was twelve and fisherman Andre saw I was getting breasts. "It's almost time, Toni, you'll need to keep the studs away."

We were standing at the quay, Andre was jabbing a needle into his torn net, while his shoulders shook with laughter. And that Andre . . . That Andre had a wife, Karla, who slept with her nephew. The boy, the son of Andre's brother, was fifteen, Karla at least thirty-five. Old Andre, who wasn't old at the time, didn't dare to tell his slut wife she was a slut, but he told my father I'd be one if he didn't keep me safe. Would my father have seen sluts in my sister and me if people hadn't told him that's what we might become? They wanted to take the boy, whom old Karla was humping, out of the claws of his lascivious aunt, so they decided to send him to school in a place some twenty miles from our hometown. That was the end of the world back then. Old Karla couldn't come to terms with it, she cried and asked to at least be allowed to say goodbye to the boy at the bus station. They agreed. When she wrapped her arms around his neck in front of his father and mother, no one knew that she was hiding a razor blade in her left hand. She slashed his face and almost blinded him. And Andre, who stayed with Karla until his death separated them, was the first to tell my father that he'd have to go from being the father of a little girl into the custodian of a slut. I'll tell you something else about that now-deceased old Karla. There wasn't much in the way of public transportation to and from our town. We girls usually hitched a ride. Old Karla did too. When dark fell, she'd stand by the roadside, raise her skirt, and show her bare leg. The car would stop, the driver would open the door, and when he saw that the owner of the leg wasn't twenty but sixty, it was too late. You get me? I didn't learn anything from old Karla. There's no way of me, today at sixty, standing by the roadside and deceiving honest men. When her granddaughter, Nancy, found her in bed with an elderly gentleman, she told her he was just rubbing her back.

Nancy said: "My God, I'll never forget that old man's withered, sagging butt as long as I live. I couldn't come for days after that. I can't have an orgasm with my eyes open anyway. I'm not exactly crazy about Joško, my husband, so I half close my eyes, and then it's someone else on top of me every time. But after that sight it was either that trembling old butt or Joško staring down at me. Jesus Christ!"

When our first day carer quit because her mother fell ill, we went hunting for another. On her recommendation we hired Kata, a lady my age, in jeans, slender, with well-groomed nails and a nice smile—a lively peroxide blonde. I told her we didn't expect her to do very much: make soup three times a week, serve it every day with rice, don't give my mother any milk or milk products, bathe her once a week, ensure she always had clean underwear and a clean tracksuit, make her get out of bed, and give her Ultram, six drops a day at most. Weekends and public holidays off, working hours from ten to two, for three hundred and fifty euros. I drove her into the city, she lives downtown, and we had coffee at the bar where my husband works as a waiter. The air was fuggy although the door stood wide open. I regret that the law banning smoking has been abolished. We sat near the door. Kata watched me with a smile. She lit up a cigarette. I didn't tell her she wasn't supposed to smoke in the apartment, but there would be time for that. Beautiful young women with bare legs went past along the street. High heels, ironed hair, sunglasses—slim, svelte, and slender. Firm and well-toned, all the girls are into sports these days. I'll buy a bike too, I thought. The young waitress looked at us with tedium. Kata asked me what I wanted. We ordered a decaf macchiato for me and an espresso for her. Two lawyers were sitting by the window. Ana always says it's very hard when you're watching the news in Croatia today to figure out who's the lawyer and who's the criminal: both have shaven heads, bodybuilder physiques, and Armani suits. These two were in cheap, gray suits. They were drinking whiskey even though it was ten in the morning.

"Gypsies never pay, I've given up on them."

"No, they're the same as everyone else. You have to make them pay in advance, and if there's a hitch later on, you can always return part of the gravy."

"I'm not going to represent them anymore. While they're in pretrial custody, their relatives keep calling, 'Doctor, Doctor, please help!' When you get the guy out of custody his whole tent throws a welcome party for him out on the road, they all cry with joy, and then the 'doctor' has to keep ringing and threatening them for months. No Gypsies or damn Albanians anymore!"

"No, come on, like I told you—," the lawyer nervously drew smoke into his lean body, "make him pay up front, and once you've got him out: goodbye."

"You mean, 'goodbye and good riddance'?"

"No, just 'goodbye for now.' When they end up in custody the next time they whine as if they've paid me—'Doctor, Doctor!'—it sure makes you feel like getting rid of them. Then again, if I get rid of the Gypsies, who will I have left? There are three lawyers in the city who make a living on the criminal cases, the rest of us have to take what's left. Dammit, when I think back to how it used to be: there were just the five of us here, and now there are three hundred and ninety."

"And the registration fee is five thousand euros."

"Yep, five thousand euros. One of my clients has been indicted for neglecting minors. I'll say to that goat of a judge: 'Your Honor, my client loves all his ten children and certainly would never leave them uncared for if he weren't constantly in jail. Besides, there was no molestation of the minors. Considering that you acquitted a Gypsy who slept with his thirteen-year-old sister-in-law because that's customary among the Gypsies, why the hell, Your Honor, are you now messing my client around' . . ."

"They really go overboard with the molestation," the lawyer in the darker gray suit said, looking at the round behind of a young woman who was making her way through to the toilet. "If my father hadn't belted me I wouldn't be what I am today. Have you noticed there are no blondes anymore, they're all jet-blacks or brunettes?"

"I like redheads, it's a shame they all shave these days, you only come across red beaver once in ten years."

"Have you heard the latest one about the blonde?" The lawyer in the dark suit wiped his glasses with a tissue.

"Fire away!"

"A blonde goes to see her gynecologist and says, 'Doctor, I have vagina pectoris.' The doctor looks at her dimly, and she starts to get uneasy. 'Why are you staring at me like that, Doctor? I have vagina pectoris, are you going to treat me or not?' And then the doctor . . ." The lawyer laughed loudly. "The doctor starts taking off his pants. The blonde goes, 'Doctor, what are you doing?' And the doctor says, 'I'm going to implant you a penis maker!'"

"Ha, ha, ha, ha," the lawyers hooted.

Kata's pink artificial nails didn't inspire much trust. Where was the money coming from? I pay three hundred kuna a week for my nails. And it's money well spent—my husband loves it when I scratch his back once a month, it's incredible how nails speed up the whole thing.

"My mother isn't really in pain, you have to bear that in mind, but phantom pain is still pain. What do I expect of you? You can make her soup on Mondays and Fridays, she'll tell you how to do it, you put a handful of rice into boiling water, that shouldn't be a problem. As soon as you get there you make her coffee and take it to her in bed, wait a little and then walk her to the toilet. Wait a minute, and when she does a number two you go in and wash her bottom with lukewarm water, the washbowl is on top of the washing machine, give her clean underwear every day, change her tracksuit, if she feels sick and needs a doctor she should be neat and tidy, put on her terry socks, check she's comfortable in them, comb what's left of her hair, then you take hold of her under the arm and go for a little stroll around the apartment with her for at least ten minutes, she hates having to move around, so be persistent."

"Don't you worry," Kata said in a cloud of smoke. "I love old folks, you've told me all that already, and I remember."

"Oh, yes, I forgot—no smoking in the apartment."

"I'll smoke out on the balcony, don't you worry, just don't you worry."

"And I haven't told you the most important thing: my mother suffers from phantom pain. She isn't really in pain, but phantom pain is still pain . . ."

"Of course, don't you worry at all," Kata said.

"I'm telling you because my mother will moan and ask for Ultram although she isn't really in pain."

"Don't you worry at all, I understand completely," Kata took her purse out of her handbag.

"No, no, that's out of the question, I'm getting this."

"All right," said Kata.

"Also, I have to ask you to insist that she put in her new teeth every day. She hates them because she says they rub, although the dentist tells me it's a phantom sensation—there's nothing rubbing. Make her read the paper every day, and you should give her a good massage at least once a day with Tiger Balm, even though she prefers Horse Balm, both are in the small cupboard in the bathroom."

"Just don't you worry, I've taken to the lady already, we'll be bosom friends."

The two lawyers ordered another round and laughed loudly when the young woman with the big ass bent over to pick up a tissue she'd dropped on the floor. We left.

"That's it, basically," I said as a young guy went past us with a bag of sweet pastries. I could have buried myself in those pastries.

Kata was staring into the window of the jewelry store. "Sorry, what did you say?"

"My mom's totally deaf from time to time, but only from time to time."

"Don't you worry at all, just don't you worry."

Kata took the bus to my mother's, and I headed home. I parked in front of the house, got out of the car, and ralphed in my neighbor's lilac bush. Was it the macchiato? The smoke? Those lawyers? Kata? Mom? Dad?

"I had a good laugh today. The psychiatrist came to see me and asked what day it is today. 'Friday,' I said. He was surprised, they think I'm crazy. How's my Rabby?"

"Mom, I'm glad you're in a good mood. Nobody thinks you're crazy, Rabby is frolicsome."

"Do you scratch her between the ears?"

"Every day."

"Do you buy parsley for her?"

"Every day."

"How often do you lie to me?"

"Every day."

She laughed.

9

My dad? why can't I clear my nose of my dead father, who simply loved me too much? I inherited a little old seaside house from him, on top of a small hill, because he died suddenly without leaving a will. I'll take you to see that house.

At the front is a stone basin full of stagnant rainwater. Lavender, rosemary, and thyme grow around the house. When you open the small front door with the clunky key, you come into a large room with rotten floorboards and an enormous hearth. My father was enchanted by everything still being like it was a hundred and fifty years earlier. On the left is a meager bedroom, in it a camp bed, and on the gnarled wall a photograph. Tito and Jovanka.

My father had gouged out Jovanka's eyes. Why not Tito's? He always said we'd be up to our knees in blood when the old swine croaked.

When I first showed the house to my husband, he shuddered when he saw Jovanka's empty eye sockets. "The poor thing," he said to me and took me by the hand, we went down the steps and lay on the grass in front of the house. We looked at the sea and the fig tree. My husband took off my white T-shirt just like I've had to take off my mother's pajama top, and I lifted my butt so he could pull off my jeans just like I've had to pull off my mother's pajama bottoms, and afterward he slipped my panties back on me just like they'll slip pale-green diapers on me one day in this home.

I tried calling her. She didn't answer.

Half an hour later I rang again. No answer this time, either.

"What's happened? My mom isn't answering!"

The head nurse laughed. "You worry too much. Today is bathing, maybe she got tired and she's sleeping, or maybe she's out walking around the home, it's a lovely day."

"Sorry, I got a fright. I thought something might have happened to her."

"Like what?"

"She could have died."

I heard the nurse giggle, her mouth must have been stretched from ear to ear. They all smile over the phone as well. "Your mom is healthy—a little depressive, but healthy. The doctor has prescribed her Prozac. It needs a bit of time, it doesn't act immediately, but then your mom will be her old self again, a cheerful woman full of life."

"Thank you," I said. "I'll call again later."

I didn't call. *She's alive, healthy, clean, and walking. I'll go to work and then spend the whole afternoon lying on the couch watching the birds as they peck at the food in the wooden birdhouse in the fig tree*, I thought. She called me, trying to get through; she called and called. I didn't answer. No one gives me Prozac to cheer me up, I'm not going to answer, no, no, no.

10

My father was like yours? Maybe.

I told my husband: "There's no way I'm going up there by myself and telling her. You do it if you dare."

"Just relax," my husband said. "She has a roof over her head, she has food, she has a good twenty people fussing over her. Why are you so stressed out? Come on, let's enjoy ourselves a bit."

"How do you mean 'enjoy ourselves a bit'? Would you be able to enjoy yourself if your mother was fading away before your eyes? If she was withering away? She's vanishing."

"Is there anything you can do about it? How do you plan to keep your mother from vanishing at the age of eighty-four? Be rational."

"You tell her, you tell her, you tell her . . ." I was trembling. He kept his hand on my knee and drove along the narrow road to the home.

We entered the building. The two men about my age raised their eyes from their newspapers and then lowered them again.

The lady with Alzheimer's said to us cheerfully: "How are you, how are you, how are you, how are you . . ."

The receptionist stretched her mouth across her face: "Hello, how are you, what a lovely day, your mother's doing fine."

We went down the immaculate marble steps of the staircase and passed through the empty restaurant with the jugs of orange liquid on the tables. I knocked on the door and entered my mother's room. The Immobile Lady was watching TV wearing only a plastic diaper and a loose-fitting pajama top.

"Hello," I said, "my husband is bringing coffee."

The Immobile Lady smiled at me and pulled the sheet up over her turquoise diaper. My mother was sleeping with her mouth open.

"How was she last night?"

"She slept all night, and she sleeps all day, too, she really can sleep, she sleeps and eats like a baby, but look at me, touch my leg . . ."

I touched her leg.

"Can you feel that?"

"Yes, I can."

The TV was blaring. The walls showed photographs of the Immobile Lady when she was young: her wedding, small children, walking by the sea with a young man, smiles, the sun in children's hair . . .

"They'd like to come but they can't make it, and my husband died. I told your mom: 'You're a lucky woman, your children are always visiting,' but in vain. They refitted her buzzer yesterday and asked her to please not badger them all the time, but as soon as the nurse went out of the room she started to yell: 'It hurts so bad, so bad, so bad . . .' Terrible. They switched off her buzzer again, and so they should have. She thinks she's the only person in the world . . ."

"What's the lady saying? That I'm pampered?"

"Mom, you're awake!" My voice sounded overjoyed.

"Awake? I haven't slept for days. What was she saying?"

"The lady said her children don't come because they have to work so much, and you're lucky because we're here every day."

"You didn't come yesterday. Or the day before."

"I was at the dentist's."

"You're always going to the dentist's."

My husband came into the room. The Immobile Lady pulled the sheet up to her neck. "Hello, how are we today?" my husband said and took her the coffee in a small plastic cup as if he was carrying an Olympic medal.

The Immobile Lady laughed and said "Hello." My mother smiled with her dark-blue lips. Her toothless gums were dark red.

"Mom, why don't you put your teeth in?"

"Don't attack me, you're always at me. I don't want the teeth, I don't need teeth when they blend up my food for me."

"If you put your teeth in you'd be able to bite and eat something normal."

"Come on, come on, leave your mom alone. Nana, why do you let your daughter mistreat you like this?"

"You're the only one who understands me, you're the only one who believes me," my mother said and once more stretched her dark-blue mouth into a grin.

"Here's the coffee."

"Raise the head end of the bed." My mother watched me with her pale-brown left eye. Her right eye was closed. I went up to the bed holding the remote. I pressed some button and her legs shot up into the air. She shrieked: "Let me down, let me down."

I shuddered and returned the bed to its normal position.

"You'll kill me, you don't know how much everything hurts."

"I'll try again."

"No!" my mother howled. "Don't touch me!"

I recoiled and stood by the bedside. She looked at me fiercely with her left eye, trying in vain to open the right eye.

"Good, Nana, you'll drink the coffee later, in peace. How are you?"

"Everything hurts, I want to die."

"You can't die as long as we love you."

"If you loved me you'd give me something to stop this pain."

"The nurses put on patches. You mustn't overdo it, otherwise the patches will totally stupefy you. You have to be alert so you can eat, recover, and come home to us . . ."

"But the pain . . ."

"I believe you," my husband stroked her left arm. "There's something I have to tell you. Tomorrow I'm going on a business trip to Kraków, and I wanted to ask you if my wife can come along with me. She doesn't want to because she thinks she has to be with you. I told her: 'Your mom understands that work is work, and I don't like traveling alone, you know that.' So I wanted to ask you . . . Would you lend me your daughter for seven days?"

My mom laughed: "Lend? She's for keeps, you don't have to give her back, you can leave her in Kraków."

"Bravo, Nana," he said.

"Just have her turn me on my side."

I turned her onto her left. She shrieked. Then onto her right. She moaned. I returned her to her original position.

"Try and get some sleep."

If looks could kill, hers would have killed me. "Tell the nurse to give me something."

"Don't worry," my husband said, "don't worry."

"Did you see that?" he asked me afterward. "You need to know how to treat her. A bit of patience and a kind word. The old woman just wants a bit of attention . . ."

"A bit of attention! I've been thinking about her and nothing else for months, day and night. She's my breakfast, lunch, and dinner. She's never satisfied, maudlin all the time, ungrateful, savage . . . I can't go on like this."

"Come on," my husband kissed me on the neck in the car. "Just think of the two of us rolling on a hotel bed hundreds of miles from the home. Enjoy life, my love."

"Let me ask you . . ."

"If my mom was in the same place as yours? Come on, leave my mom out of it."

Kraków is a wonderful city, maybe our favorite. I love Warsaw too. Two years ago I came across a souvenir shop there. It sells wooden angels in all sizes and colors, as well as zany Jesuses. The one I liked most was a wooden Christ climbing up a wooden ladder onto the cross. Suddenly I had an idea. How a look through a shopwindow can change your life!

From Warsaw we traveled by Intercity. Drinks and sandwiches were sold by magnificent, blond, blue-eyed Polish women without a trace of makeup.

"Why are such beautiful girls doing menial work like this? They should go to Hollywood."

"No idea." My husband was reading a detective novel, while I looked out the window. A boundless landscape, no houses or people anywhere, only huge, dark trees; that's how the world would look after the Americans and Israelis nuke Iran, if Iran really does have the Bomb.

Going to Kraków is like entering a fairy tale. A large paved square with coaches, horses, and old houses, the Jewish Quarter. Our friend lives right on the square in an enormous building, once expropriated but recently returned. She also owns the cinema on the second floor and all the bars and restaurants on the first floor. A friend of hers owns the best restaurant in Kraków, and she invited us to dinner. About twenty women and three men were seated at the tables. The proprietress's boyfriend kissed my hand—she was sixty, he seventeen. I pretended it didn't surprise me at all. She went around the tables, welcomed the guests, and came back to us to hold out her aged neck to her tender young sweetheart for a kiss. I was the only one who wasn't knocking back one vodka after another. I watched the boy: delicate, in a black suit and white shirt, with a beardless, pale face, dense dark-brown hair slicked back, large dark eyes, and a full, rosy mouth. What did this woman my age see in him, and he in her? How could she be so relaxed and hug the boy and kiss him on the temple? Did the lady have a mom? And where was she?

"Where is your mother, and how is she?" I asked the owner of the restaurant.

"I beg your pardon?" she replied in perfect English.

I said to her in my English: "My mom is ill, she's in a home, that's why I'm asking about your mom. I'm always thinking about mine."

My husband looked at me in dismay.

"She's probably at home, I haven't seen her for months."

"Do you phone?" I was persistent.

"No," came the curt reply, and her young beau smiled at me.

The ladies were soon drunk. All of them were attractive and, with the exception of the proprietress, very young. I said to my husband: "Let's go to the hotel, I'm tired."

We left and started across the square toward the hotel. It was called The White Rose. The owner ordered fresh roses from Holland every day.

"Why the talk about your mom?" my husband asked as we ran, arm in arm, to avoid the horses and coaches.

"I don't know, I keep thinking about her. It's stronger than me. That Polish woman isn't normal—what does she see in that boy? Her sixty, him perhaps seventeen . . ."

My husband stared at me, his eyes laughing.

"That 'boy' isn't a boy, he's a girl in a suit. Magda told me."

I stopped short, and a stout, white horse almost ran me down. My husband pulled me away to the side.

"A girl?"

"Yes, a girl. That woman sure knows how to enjoy life."

We went into the hotel and into the most beautiful room in the world with a view of that fairy-tale square crawling with hordes of drunken British. They come to Kraków on charter flights on weekends to celebrate their birthdays. My husband came out of the bathroom naked. I went in: a crystal mirror, marble, a glass bath, thick, white towels, and a thick, white dressing gown. I came back to the room naked and lay on the bed, he turned me on my side, and I heard him groan. The Brits laughed, the horses whinnied, and my mom watched me with her left eye.

We got up early in the morning and looked for the museum where Leonardo da Vinci's *Girl with a Lamb* was on show. I'm not crazy about museums, although I've been to all of the major European exhibitions. There isn't a Van Gogh I haven't stared at from up close. But actually I'm not so fond of exhibitions, I prefer the museum shops where I always buy a magnet to put on the fridge to remind me how sophisticated I am. We really looked hard. The Poles we met had never heard of Leonardo's girl with a lamb. They looked at us wide-eyed when I pretended to be rocking a lamb in my arms. I bleated: "Baa, baa, da Vinci." We ran into a Brit who understood both "Leonardo da Vinci" and "baa, baa," and so we finally found the museum. It was not much more than five hundred square feet in size, and we were alone as we admired *The Lady with an Ermine*. Where did I get the idea the woman was holding a young sheep? It's the most beautiful picture in the world. We stood there in front of it for half an hour because there were no impatient Japanese tourists breathing down our necks.

"It's so beautiful," I said to my husband. "Let's go to the shop for a magnet."

There was no shop and no magnet. I'm glad no one told the Japanese that Leonardo da Vinci and the lady with the ermine are hanging in Kraków all on their own. I didn't tell my husband that the ermine looked at me with the eyes of my mom.

"When did you come back?"

"Last night."

"Why didn't you call?"

"In the middle of the night?"

"How many days has Rabby been without parsley?"

"Tiny looked after her."

"When are you coming?"

"Tomorrow."

"When tomorrow?"

"When would it suit you?"

"Come as soon as you can."

"Why?"

"So I can see you one more time before I die."

"Don't exaggerate, Mom. Who knows who'll be the first to go. The nurses say you're recovering well."

"When did they say that?"

"Before we went on our trip."

"Enjoy life while you can, my daughter, and when you get to my age pay someone to kill you."

"Mom, cheer up a bit, we're all fussing over you, we all love you—my husband and Tiny and me . . ."

"You too?"

"Yes, me too. And we can all hardly wait for you to get better so you can leave this Center for . . ."

"Center for Dying."

"Come on, calm down now. Sleep tight."

I hung up.

11

It was two years ago that we returned from Poland to a depressive Croatia in the grip of animal flus. With a chubby wooden angel in my bag. Angels bring good luck and look after the house. Each of us has a guardian angel . . . Do we? How can people know they have a guardian angel if they can't take it in their hand? I'll keep it brief. My chubby angel made me cheerful and calm, and why should I alone be cheerful and calm in Croatia? Happiness ought to be shared and spread. Guardian angels have to be made of wood.

Wood is a noble material, always warm to the touch. It would be silly to have an angel at home made of iron, stainless steel, or plastic. Metal is cold, and plastic reminds you of China. No one wants a Chinese caretaker in a house already populated by Chinese toys, T-shirts, Armani suits, tea sieves, potato mashers, light fixtures, tablecloths, bedside lamps, living-room lamps, rakes, spades, picture frames, kitchen trays, glasses, plates with matching place mats, TVs, cars, caps, gloves, undies, panties, long johns, shoes, pantyhose, hand-painted frozen prawns . . . I drove to my native town. Everything's still as it was when I was twelve and went to the park with Dad. The park is a little way from the town center. When you turn off the main road, at the best fish restaurant, called Marina, the first thing you'll see will be a large, dark-yellow villa, sixty or so years old. It was built by a husband and wife who collected aid in America for Yugoslav orphans during the Second World War. Whether they really plowed all the aid money into that luxurious house, or only a smaller part and kept the rest in cash, was never known. To the left of the villa is the hotel whose grounds were tended by my father. Have I told you he was a gardener? Such a good gardener that one of his dark-green walls, to the right of the hotel entrance, was included in *The Encyclopedia of Gardening*, as published in Yugoslavia. There's a small church in the center of the town, as tiny as can be. All the locals have always gone to church every Sunday and sung. My father, mother, grandma, and sister never set foot in that building. I did, once, Silvana took me. My father found out and gave me a belting. Only a belting. I was eight at the time. There's a fountain in the square. A big rosebush grows at the edge of the fountain, and a different-colored rose flowers on every branch. Dark red, yellow, pink, pale red, white . . . My father was an artist, he really had a green thumb.

You can go down to the lovely pebbly beach either through the hotel or over the square. The largest beach is down to the right of the square, but it's not the most beautiful one. To the left of the square is the Bar. When I lived there, which was for eighteen years, women weren't allowed to enter the Bar. They just drank coffee at the little cafe in the market. But at home there was rum. They hit the booze at home while their husbands got drunk at the Bar. The little port is lovely: wooden fishing boats, nets used to be out drying at the quay, a fish market in a stone building by the side of the road that leads toward the park. If you want to get to the most beautiful beach, you have to walk along the edge of the largest one. In socialist times, the first building on the right was the police station. Today it's just an ordinary house that's been bought up by Slovenians. Not five minutes' walk and you come to a huge stone monument. This is where a number of war heroes once landed and were probably killed; if they'd survived, there wouldn't be a big stone standing there. To the right of the narrow path is a beach, another beach, and yet another, and then a villa like something out of a dream. It was probably in a place like this that the prince woke that pale girl. The villa is surrounded by a sea of pebbles. A real manor, and separated from us mortals by an iron fence. Yugoslav politicians and their children vacationed here in the old days. Today a Russian periodically resides here; he declares for the newspapers that he loves art. And there are the cliffs, the sea, cypresses, stone pines, rosemary, and strange plants whose names I don't know. My father planted all of them. On Sundays, when the most people went walking there, he'd take care that women not break off sprigs of those exotic plants.

"You bitch!" he used to snarl at each of them he caught in the act. "Bitch!" He'd snatch the sprig out of her hand and gently lay it beside the mother plant.

Bougainvillea grows in front of my house. A gigantic bush. Some bitches think that if they break off a branch and put it in water, it will develop roots. Stupid bitches. I see them doing their bit of vandalism. I don't say anything, I just go out in front of the house, take the branch of bougainvillea out of their hands, and gently lay it next to the mother bougainvillea. What bitches! At the very end of the short walk, if you cock your head to one side, you'll see a narrow little path that leads to the most beautiful beach. Tall rocks rise up above the beach. I used to jump from them into the sea when I was a girl.

The woodworking shop is at the opposite end of the town, beside the park. You can go there by car. The road is wide. The workshop is separated from it by a steep set of stairs. I went into the workshop, expecting to see Stanko there. I didn't know that six months earlier Stanko had dressed up as a nun, got in his wooden go-kart, and been killed. I don't read death notices or the local paper. In fact, I don't read any newspapers at all. The workshop smelled of my childhood. The enormous high ceiling, sawdust, doors, windows, boards, and weird machines, but I didn't see any coffins. If I'd seen at least one, I would have lain in it and looked up through the large skylight. And there in the corner, by the big window, stood Ana, the mother of little Jerry. We gave birth in the maternity hospital together thirty years ago.

When the baby came, the nurse asked Ana what she was going to call her son.

"Jerry," Ana said.

"Jerry?" the nurse was baffled by the name. "Er, is that with a G or a J?"

"Jerry with a J."

Ana was the young mother they examined the most. The gynecologists kept uncovering her bronzed body and feeling her abdomen to see if she was bleeding or not. Even the students came and inspected her. Ana used to sunbathe naked on the beach while the rest of us hid our bulges in dresses as wide as tents. Today's expectant moms sport their pregnant bellies wearing thin T-shirts. And the dads of this new generation treat their partners' baby bumps as a claim to fame. Perhaps aided by the fact that ever less people can have children. Back then, we kittened like it was going out of fashion.

"Hello? Hello?" my mother snarled into the phone.

"Hello? Hello?" I shouted in the voice of a child.

"Who's that there?" My mother changed her voice, "Who's speaking?"

"Hello? Hello?" I shouted in the voice of a five-year-old girl.

"Sorry, darling," my mom said.

She called my cell phone. I answered and screamed the same thing into it, but I forgot to disguise my voice. She hung up.

12

My mother called me about twenty years ago: "Come and get me!"

I went into her house, my father was nowhere to be seen. She was sitting in the kitchen on a fat black sack, and I didn't know what was inside it. It looked like a misshapen fitness ball, I think when I look back today. When my mother sat on that sack, fitness balls had yet to be invented. I felt a bit strange. How had it come to this all of a sudden? Was she leaving? War was about to break out, and we didn't know what we were going to do—flee or stay in Croatia. Tiny was a little girl.

"Come and get me," she said.

My husband has always been a good man. I don't know if I'd have been so quick to help his mom if she decided to leave her husband one day, God forbid. As soon as my mother saw me, she grabbed the fat black sack nervously, really nervously. I snatched it out of her hand to help her. It was light.

"What's inside?"

"A pillow and medicines."

"How long do you think you'll stay?" I asked as I stuffed the sack onto the back seat of the baby Fiat.

"I'm never coming back."

"I'm well today, I ate my greens and walked around the institution. In one room the therapist and I saw bedridden old people. It was a terrible sight. They stare at the wall with their eyes wide open, lying on their backs, legs up in the air, and their arms, too. The therapist said it's paralysis. Today I took off my diaper and went to the toilet by myself."

"Bravo, Mom!"

"The pain's getting less, it only hurts at the top on the left, but it's getting less. You can come and drive me home."

"I'll talk to the doctor."

I hung up. Tiny birds were pecking at the food in the red wooden birdhouse. Perhaps it was a good idea: I'd take her back to my place, tell her she could go back to her apartment when she recovered a bit more, and then one evening I'd tip the three bottles of Ultram down her throat—the ones that Tiny and I had found hidden in an old light fixture at the bottom of the wardrobe.

13

"Traveling titillates the soul," my husband likes to say. Who knows if we'd be able to titillate our souls and pay for the home for my mother if we hadn't stumbled across the wooden-angel shop that day in Warsaw.

I asked Ana how Jerry and Stanko were. She told me about Stanko being killed. I didn't get the impression she was overly sad; Jerry was well.

"I run the business now. All the plastic on the market hasn't ruined us yet. People still love wood."

Ana looked fantastic: slim, with jeans and a white T-shirt. Short hair, dark eyes, a pale face, a full mouth, beautiful teeth, and a neck that erased at least fifteen years.

"I can't believe it!" I exclaimed. "You're just the same."

"The same," Ana said and laughed, "just thirty years older. Maybe Stanko's death rejuvenated me."

"How do you mean?"

"He used to beat me, he broke my arm, and look at this . . ."

She pushed back her short hair. I saw a long scar as thin as a hair. A knife? I don't watch crime shows.

"If you want, I can show you my thighs. He used to stub out cigarettes on them."

"No, don't show me your thighs. Why didn't you leave?"

"Where to?"

"Anywhere, you could have gone to Italy to find work. Or you could have killed him."

"And never see Jerry again . . . In Croatia, if a woman kills her abusive husband and eventually gets released from prison, they ban her from coming back to her hometown, and they take away her child. In Croatia, all women who resist their abusive husbands are treated like witches, without exception. Only men have a right to use knives, guns, mallets, and burning cigarettes. Don't you read the papers?"

"No, I don't."

I had no idea what she was talking about. I don't read the newspapers because I can't bear all the reports about violence. I'm not interested in how many people were killed in Iraq or how many women have been beaten, shot, strangled, raped, and slaughtered in Croatia in just one day. It disturbs me too much.

"We're a wild country," I said. "We can't become like Sweden overnight."

"There's just a handful of houses in Croatia where beaten women can flee to. Sweden has over a hundred women's shelters. That just means that the Swedes take better care of their battered women. The world isn't divided into Croatians and Swedes in terms of violence against women. All countries are Croatia when a man clenches his fist or takes a knife and attacks a woman, who for him is a piece of meat with a hole in the middle. Stanko was terrible. I'm glad he was so nuts about carnival."

"If that's the way it is, Ana—enjoy!"

"I am enjoying it," she laughed.

I explained what I wanted and asked if she could make a fat wooden angel with a large head. The cheeks had to be chubby, it needed to have a full-lipped smile and sweet little eyes. "And it shouldn't be too small, life-size would be best . . ."

"What's life-size for an angel?" Ana chuckled.

"Twenty inches."

"Will do."

"But you said you took off your diaper."

"It's still too early to go without diapers," the voice in the receiver was that of a woman who knew what she wanted.

"Mom, it's stupid for you to be wearing diapers, especially when you were looking after yourself until just yesterday. The doctors say you can go to the toilet yourself without any trouble. You can call a nursing attendant if you feel unsteady on your legs . . ."

"They've switched off my buzzer."

"Mom, the diapers cost us a thousand three hundred kuna per month, that's no small money today."

"You can pay for them out of my pension. The masseur and the therapist came today. If you insist I practice walking in the afternoon, too, you'll have to pay two kuna per minute."

14

I FELT GOOD when I came out of the workshop. A beautiful spring morning. The sea was a Paris blue, a few men were fishing from the quay. Why not head toward the park and have a look at the window where old Katica lived? She was the only one in town who had begonias. Were they flowering already? It was April. Today I know what I didn't back then, when I admired the beautiful dark-red flowers as a girl: begonias don't tolerate full sun. Except those called Dragon Wing, but there weren't any of them back then. I only discovered them recently. If I'd known when I was small how hard it is to keep begonias in a bright, sunny place, I might remember what the late Katica looked like. I headed for the park. The window of Katica's house was bare. A young woman at the front door was trying to calm a red-haired baby and cooed to it in Italian, but it bawled and showed the world its four teeth. Was that the new owner of the house, or just a guest? Who does the house belong to today? Katica didn't have any children. I entered the park. The trail was covered with gravel. The iron fence separating the little path from the jagged rocks wound and bent wickedly. I didn't feel anything. I made for the bench. And sat down on it. Trauma? How long does trauma last? Anxiety? Regret? Anger? Powerlessness? Sorrow? Self-pity? Had I studied literature, I'd know. But I didn't. I sat on that bench and remembered the time my father . . . How many years ago was that? I was twelve. Sixty minus twelve . . . Forty-eight years ago my father placed his big paw between my skinny legs. I recoiled and squeezed them together, but he roughly prized them apart and put his hand there again. Firmly. He pressed against me. And looked out to sea. Somebody on a boat threw a net into the water. When the boat came closer to the park, we saw it was Uncle Dino. How many seconds, minutes, or hours did Father keep his hand between my legs? I don't know. Was that molestation? He didn't rape me, he just kept his hand there, squeezing tight, so firmly that I was unable to move.

Uncle Dino came right up close in his boat. "Hi," he called to us.

"Hi," Dad and I said.

"My blood pressure is normal." Her face was covered with red spots. I stood next to the window holding a cup of coffee from the vending machine. "I didn't get a wink of sleep all night, the pain is killing me, but they don't give me anything to stop it."

"Mom, they're putting on patches, but they're taking care that you don't get an overdose."

"How could I? The patches don't work, why don't they give me something, I didn't get a wink of sleep all night . . ."

"She's lying," the Immobile Lady said, "she slept the whole night. I was awake, my legs are like posts, I can't feel them at all, I lie awake every night, ask the nurses if you don't believe me."

"What's that lady saying? That I'm bad? I'm a good old woman—good and patient. Why don't they give me some drops?"

15

My mother lay down on the couch in the living room, her back was hurting.

"A baby Fiat is an uncomfortable car," she said.

"You can sleep here on the couch. I'll sleep with the others in the bedroom, some of us can go on the floor."

"You make me feel guilty," my mother said, "I can sleep on the floor even though my back hurts."

We lived in a one-bedroom apartment with a living room. Life wasn't easy. Less and less people frequented the bar where my husband worked as a waiter, and the heroes in camouflage uniforms never paid for their drinks. Refugees were housed in the hotel where I used to work at the reception desk. They were nervous and also furious that their relatives from Slavonia would always call when they weren't in their room. I breathed a sigh of relief when I was given notice. I went to coach school students in German. At the time, people thought a knowledge of foreign languages would be their children's salvation. Fortunately, very few people in Croatia speak German, so my students' parents couldn't check up on me. I spoke German excellently once, but that was long ago. I felt a need to talk with my mother in peace. Without my husband and without Tiny. We went to the bar in front of our building. The chestnut trees were enormous, it was summer, and Mom and I were in short sleeves. My mother didn't care about the loose skin on her upper arms the way I'm bothered by mine today. Beauty meant nothing to her. She always stressed that there had never been rouge on her lips or cream on her skin. Back then, when we sat under those chestnut trees and ordered coffee. She a cappuccino, I a macchiato. Actually, there's no chance in the world I could ever remember the details of what we ordered. I just mentioned those coffees so it wouldn't sound as if we were sitting there without anything on the table in front of us, we were at the bar, after all. I remember what we said, not what we ordered, but I realize the story will be more lively if I mention our short sleeves and coffees. The waiter, let's say it was Željko, brought us our coffees. Today he works on an oil rig, and I ask myself how he copes—he's not young anymore like he was when the war was about to break out. Željko was tall, slim, and had eyes the color of water. I'm not saying it was him who served us; even if it was, my mother wouldn't have said: "How handsome that man is," she always made it a point that men didn't mean anything to her.

My mother's skin is as white as that of a nun who never goes to the beach. I'd have no idea what her skin was like if I hadn't watched them turning, wiping, and massaging her in the home . . . An ancient baby without the right to bawl or shout, even when the diaper changes and massages are unpleasant and painful for her. When she started groaning—and she groaned every time a nursing attendant turned her from one side to the other—they always said to her: "Come on, Grandma, don't be so spoilt, just put up with it a tiny bit more. You have to be good or you'll get sores, and what will we do with you then?"

"Why can't I die?" my mother asked me loudly as the unfamiliar woman adjusted her blanket.

I stood smiling at the bedside. "Because you're actually quite healthy. You aren't in pain, the pain you're feeling is phantom pain . . ."

My mother's eyes were full of tears. "You don't believe me."

"Now, now, Granny, don't be so tough on your daughter. If all daughters were like yours there would be no unhappy moms, you see how often she visits you, your son-in-law brings you coffee from the vending machine, and you keep complaining . . ."

"When I'm in pain."

"We all have pain, your daughter too, isn't that right . . ."

"That's right," I said to please the aggressive nursing attendant in the pink coat, almost forgetting that I paid thousands of kuna for every movement she made; perhaps I could have taken my mother's side in some things after all, however feigned the pain was. But I had decades of experience with doctors who are always gods, always right, and always underpaid, and that's why we patients feel guilty. Beset by that guilt inherited from the socialist system, I forgot that nothing was free anymore in that lovely home. We paid almost nine thousand kuna a month, so I was under no obligation to smile at the nurse or the attendant and, just to please them, growl at my old mom who wasn't in pain. But the psychiatrist, whom I paid separately, said she was in pain after all because phantom pain is still pain. We also paid extra for the Prozac that didn't act immediately, but they were sure it would take effect in a month or two, or three or four. I watched my withered mother in her light-green plastic diaper. It was hot, so she uncovered her spindly legs, her feet in pink slippers, and she seemed to have shrunk, her skinny torso swimming in a white undershirt. She looked at me searchingly, as if she'd discover the answer in my eyes to the question she didn't ask. *Why can't I die, what's the point of this?*

"Come on, Granny, don't mope, there's no dying before your time." The nursing attendant covered her up with the lilac-colored blanket.

"That's right, no dying before your time," I said and even pulled my mother's big toe.

She jerked her little foot away from my hand, full of disgust.

16

Two years ago, or maybe three, it was hard to find business premises in our city center. I was after something on the first floor, with an area of maybe three hundred and fifty square feet. I thought it would be ideal to have the shop near the Verbum bookstore. If customers went into the bookstore looking for a rosary, a prayer book, or a large plaster cross adorned with stylized Croatian interlace, it would hardly be a problem for them to come into my wooden-angel shop immediately next door.

"Are you crazy?" said Natali, the waitress who works with my husband. Have I mentioned that the bar is smack dab in the center of town, between the court, the jail, the police, and the Church of St. Hieronymus? "If you plan to sell anything you have to be close to a store that people are constantly going into," and she handed me the local newspaper, though I never read it.

"There are no markets in the inner city anymore," I said, "they've all been swallowed up by the shopping malls."

"What markets? The only stores that consistently do well are the ones with baby things. You know, where they sell strollers, playpens, cots, baby shirts, little dresses and caps, miniature hunting suits, pink crinolines, silver dresses for the first New Year's Eve party—that's where you should have the shop. Tights for a three-month-old baby cost seventy kuna, then they give you a fifty-percent discount. However poor people are, they can't resist buying junk like that for their babies."

I'd be lying if I said we were "lucky." My husband is an excellent waiter, and the owner of his bar is as good to him as if he was his own son. The man can't accept that he has four daughters. It was he who found a space for us next to the Happy Baby shop: one hundred and sixty square feet plus a tiny bathroom. In the meantime, Ana made thirty-two twenty-inch angels, as well as forty little six-inch angels.

"People haven't got the bread these days, and you can't leave the poor without protectors."

The angels seemed strange to me. "They lack something," I told her, "they look like boiled babies. I can't imagine anything like that protecting me and my family."

Ana laughed. She smiled often. I have good teeth, that's not the problem, but I usually don't feel like showing them. "Babe, the angels just need color. Once their faces are pink, their bodies purple, their eyes blue, their tufts of hair green, their nails dark red, their lips black, and their little teeth white, everyone will believe in their power."

"Who'll paint them?"

"I'll get back to you in a day or two."

She called me: "Babe, I've found just the right man."

I was startled when I first saw Pino in his wheelchair. I've always had trouble approaching disabled people as if they're not disabled. Pino threw me into the pits of awkwardness. It's a shame you don't know him. Down to the waist, he's a wonderful man: short, black hair tapered to a brush, or a ridge of bristles, to be exact, big brown eyes, high cheekbones, a large, straight nose, healthy teeth, broad shoulders, a muscular torso, and a pair of shorts covering his legs—or the small part that's left of his upper thighs. Who carried him up the stairs to the workshop? Where did he lose his legs, and how? Diabetes? The carnival? I went up to him as if he had legs and offered him my hand. I smiled when he grasped my small hand in his. What a handsome man, I thought. If he had legs, if he could stand, I'd probably go and snuggle up to him.

"Ana speaks very highly of you. I can hardly wait to see your first angel."

"I'll do my best."

Ana saw me out.

"What happened to his legs? Not another carnival accident?"

"No, he was a policeman, with two small children, a salary of just four thousand kuna, and constantly on the road," Ana explained. "He found a connection and went to Afghanistan. Croatians aren't involved in the fighting, and the dough is pretty substantial. A wife at home gets five thousand kuna a month, and the men on assignment get a hundred euros a day, I think. He found out after the fact that he'd have to pay a massive slug of tax on both the base wage and the per diems. They couldn't even get a shirt there, the storeroom only had size thirty-seven . . ."

Ana found out all this when she googled "Croatians in Afghanistan" or something like that. She didn't want to pay him too much.

"How did he lose his legs if he wasn't in the war?"

"I forget, maybe there was some explosion at the camp, or a stray grenade came rolling up between his legs, no idea."

"That's terrible," I said. "If you think he's good, and if work takes off, we'll pay him as if he was in Afghanistan, no per diems, naturally."

"Of course, no per diems," Ana agreed.

A tuft of dark-red hair, a little orange face, green eyes beneath black brows, a little green mouth, and a body the color of cyclamen. Our first angel.

"You're mine," I shrieked, "you're mine!"

Pino watched me from his wheelchair. "I'm glad you like it. A bit of color never hurts."

"Pino," I kissed him, "you're a genius!" I held out my hand to congratulate him, he gave me his, and the angel that was on his lap fell to the floor with a crash. Its head stayed on its shoulders.

"Good that it's made of solid wood—you can emphasize that to the customers."

When work started we came up with ever better and better ideas. Silver angels looked after people at Christmas, golden ones in the days of swine flu. No, they didn't have a little piglet painted on the ankle. That would have taken Pino too long.

Ana suggested a little bird.

"No, bird flu doesn't cut ice anymore. We can't enter the market with outmoded merchandise. Swine flu is the menace of the day. But if you insist, it won't be a problem. If you really want, every angel can have a red piglet on its little foot, too."

Pino did wonderful paintings of the sea, olive trees, rosemary bushes, and the island you could see when you opened the door of the workshop. Painting was Pino's greatest and perhaps only passion.

"Don't go to too much trouble with the piglets, Pino," I said. "There's space on the little golden tummy for the red letters . . ."

As improbable as it may sound, none of us three knew the proper name for swine flu. We googled "swine flu," and out came H1N1. The internet is a marvel. When we have dinners together, my equals in age and I often don't know when Kennedy was assassinated, when James Dean had his fatal smashup, or when the pop singer Anica Zubović was born, who recently gave a concert in Opatija. It was in the paper. Old Anica often exits the nursing home, goes up on stage, and then returns to the home. All of us had old parents, all of us wanted them to be involved in a concert or an exhibition somewhere, to enroll in a dance class instead of rotting in a blue funk. We googled "Anica Zubović born . . ." She was born on March 28, 1932, in Zagreb.

The angel business turned out to be a big hit. Not everyone was able to buy a life-size angel of solid wood, so my shop assistant Pavica and I—me in the morning, she in the afternoon—also had plyboard angels of all sizes on sale. They were much cheaper. Angels with outspread wings sold best. The outspread wings were also Pino's idea.

"They look like bats," Ana said.

"Call it artistic license," Pino sniggered

The wings were made of wire, chicken feathers, knitting needles, white wool, cuttlefish bones, and bits of a peacock feather we got from the Brionian Islands, plucked from the tail of Tito's own peacock. I've told you where the shop is, look for Happy Baby, and it's next door. We don't have a website because we can't make enough angels to keep up with demand, and I really don't want to work more or earn too much money. Ana and Pino aren't money-grubbers either. We enjoy the work, and the dough is secondary. We were very lucky with Pavica. I don't like tall, slim saleswomen with silicone breasts. They scare me. Pavica is a warm woman who knows how to explain what a wooden angel can do for a person of good will. Just between us, the mayor's office ordered three life-size angels yesterday. He's going to give two of them to other mayors who are coming to visit our city and keep one for himself.

I told his secretary: "If we're going to be giving away three life-size angels, of solid wood and hand-painted—you know how much they cost—why can't the mayor at least reduce our rent?"

"I'll ask him. I saw that you also have small plyboard angels. I've just become a grandmother to a little girl. How much are the smallest plyboard ones?"

"Ten euros plus VAT."

"I'll think about it."

I didn't want to have to give her an angel too. The angels were a real boon for me. If it hadn't been for them, my mother wouldn't have been able to stay in the most expensive home in Croatia; it has an Italian name because the proprietors aimed to cater to elderly Italians—maybe that's why they jacked up the prices. When elderly Croats came, it was too late to lower them. "My mother deserves it," I told my friends, who were appalled by the expense.

"Today I ate Chocolino crispies, drank two coffees with chocolate, a bit of iced tea, and water. For lunch I ate a whole bowl of greens, fruit yogurt, and I'll be having Chocolino again tonight."

"Bravo," I said.

"My hemorrhoids are killing me, but I went to the toilet and did a number two by myself all the same. I only just managed to drag myself there and back, only just."

"Bravo," I said.

"Buy me Faktu hemorrhoid cream."

"Bravo," I said.

The bathroom was enormous and faultlessly clean, it always had toilet paper, liquid soap, and paper napkins; every time I visited my mother, I'd go there to pee. The nursing attendants were convinced I was checking the cleanliness, but actually I have a bladder problem that simply won't go away.

"Do you know what I dreamed last night?"

"No."

"That I was in my room with my blanket over me. There was a small pot of black coffee on my night table. Rabby jumped up onto the bed, and then I woke up."

"A lovely dream. If you eat and walk a lot you can come back home, but for now just get some sleep," I shouted into the receiver.

"What's the time?"

"Five in the afternoon."

"Is that all?"

"That's all."

17

"I'M STAYING WITH you." My mother looked at me with her light-brown eyes, out under the chestnut trees at that bar. It's hard today to describe the horror that engulfed me in that first instant. But then I relaxed. I had an idea, and my mother would either accept it or she wouldn't. I had a plan and was ready to hear what she had to say.

"Why are you leaving him?"

"I can't stay there anymore, my daughter."

My daughter? How pathetic. My mother had been jittery all her life, on the edge of her nerves, full of simmering anger, at times quiet, helpless, and trembly . . . But cheap pathos like this? Never, absolutely never.

"I've had enough of it all. If you can be happy—I can too."

"Mom," I said, of all things. I never used to call her "Mom," and I don't remember having uttered it more than three times in my life, perhaps twice in the hospital while the doctors and nurses were watching me, so they'd hear we were related.

One of my friends is a doctor and she'd said: "When the doctors come up to the poor old thing's bed, make sure you're respectful, don't lose your patience, don't treat your mom like she's a retarded, fidgety child. Doctors don't like that. If they see that you care for her, they will too. But take care that your mom is clean, both body and hair, make sure she smells nice, talcum her, and say 'Mom' to her."

But to say "Mom" to her in a normal situation . . . never. Not on your life. Sitting outside that bar, I said: "Mom, if you're really thinking of leaving him, you have to know—it costs five hundred deutschmarks a month."

"Hello? Hello? Hello?" she wheezed into the receiver.

"Hello? Hello?" I yelled. "Who's calling, the phone's not working, who's calling?"

"It's me, I'm calling. Is anyone coming today?"

"Hello, hello, who's calling?"

She hung up. My cell phone rang. I'd tell her tonight that our phone wasn't working, that I'd left my cell phone in the bathroom, and that I'd been at the shop all day.

18

Twenty years passed. How incredible that sounds to me today!

"It costs five hundred marks a month."

Back then, in the prewar days, you could rent a nice apartment, eat, drink, dress, and ride the bus for five hundred marks a month. Where have those lovely, lovely days gone? Nobody ever told us the truth about the euro. When I just remember how those who rule the world doubled all the prices overnight by the introduction of the euro, I'm not at all sorry that we'll soon see all the European cities in flames. Boys and girls are already setting fire to the banks, shops, cars . . . May they set them all alight. If you ask me, the nursing homes should be the very first to go up in flames, but no one ever asks me.

"Buy me drops for my gums, buy me tissues, buy me baby cream, buy me peach tea in little bottles, and buy me straws. Why does everyone die, but I can't?"

19

"How did you arrive at that amount? Five hundred marks is a heap of money. I'm modest, I don't need much, I have my clothes, I have to go and get them, I don't eat much, I eat like a bird, I haven't got long to go . . ."

Like I said, my mother wasn't usually one for pathos like this. Her little fists lay on the wooden table and a network of dark-blue veins stood out.

"I'm not saying you've got long to go, but it's possible you could live another fifteen years . . ."

My mother laughed and revealed her ancient dentures. She'd often say they'd served her superbly for thirty years. A few years later a dentist made new false teeth for her, which she only put in on her birthdays and when she went into town.

"What are you talking about? Fifteen years? My daughter, you need your head examined."

To be quite exact, when I said, "I'm not saying you've got long to go, but it's possible you could live another fifteen years," I didn't say *live* but used the expression *make it.* I was sure she wouldn't make it that long. She was gaunt and made a weary impression, but it was probably the first time in her life that she knew what she wanted.

"You cost five hundred marks. One hundred and fifty for the apartment, and the rest for bills, food, and medicine. Freedom isn't cheap, hon, so let's go the whole hog: Father has two pensions, an Italian and a Croatian one. Have him give you one of them, we'll find some way to make up the rest, or else . . ."

"Or else what?" my mother asked.

"Or else you sell the house. I mean, you inherited it from your mother—it's not as if it's an acquisition during the marriage. He's living in *your* house. I don't want to live with you and have to wait till you die to get my share that might perhaps cover your upkeep, and might not. After all, like I say, I don't have that sort of money. If I did, maybe I'd buy you your freedom."

"Maybe?" my mother scoffed.

"Maybe," I confirmed.

The phone rang long and hard. And then my cell phone. I sat on the terrace and watched the fog devouring the church tower. A young woman had been killed in our city, kicked to death by three boys the same age. We live in a time when only the young die.

20

I'm not saying our angels are cheap, but they're not overly expensive either. When we have a sale, always just before Christmas, the smallest angels are ten percent cheaper if you pay cash, and five percent if you pay by card. Of course, I feel awkward at us selling angels more cheaply right at Christmas, but we can't be different from the others. Christmas charity only makes sense if it's explicit. The Church, philanthropists, tycoons, mayors—they all only give to the poor at Christmas if cameras are rolling. Philanthropists are only as great as the number of cameras recording their acts of charity. I don't like it, but I've never been one to swim against the stream. That's why at Christmas our angels are "a real bargain," as Pavica often says. She has a big house on the outskirts and is originally from Slovenia. It was her idea that we extend our range to include angels in the shape of Maya the Honey Bee. She bought a wooden Maya the Bee on a long stick in front of a shopping mall in Kozina. You plant the stick in the ground in a windy spot and Maya waves her little wings. Ana made ten bee-angels, and Pino painted them yellow with black stripes. The stick is Denver blue. They don't sell very well, so they're on special. Tiny thinks that's because our customers are city people, all of them live in apartments, and those who have houses prefer concrete swans with a hole under their necks or ferocious stone lions with roaring jaws. In my garden a red angel whirls its lilac-colored wings. I don't like yellow. No, it wasn't the angels that helped us move from our one-room concrete hole in the most polluted part of the city to this lovely little house in an exclusive suburb. Here I have everything I love: pictures, flowers, and a small wooden birdhouse up in the fig tree; whenever I'm at home I watch the birds going into it and carrying the food away in their beaks to their nests nearby. Am I repeating myself? Have I already mentioned those little birds? My happiness would be complete, I used to think while the birds fluttered around me, if God called my mother to Him. She vehemently refuses to believe in God, which is perhaps why He doesn't want her. Why does my mother senselessly suck minced meat through a straw into her toothless mouth day after day? Is there any justice in this world? Why don't I, her sixty-year-old child, have the right to some peace of mind? Will I have to pay for the rest of my life for the staff of the most expensive home in this country to strive to keep my mother alive, against her will and mine? Everyone talks about the extension of people's life span as a miracle we ought to rejoice at. The extension of some people's life is a killing of other people in their best years.

"Hello? Hello? Hello?"

"It's me. What's troubling you?"

"What's troubling me? My daughter, everything's troubling me. Are any of you coming today?"

"Why?"

"To see me."

"Mom, we saw you yesterday. We were all there, remember?"

"Please come today and bring me the ointment, I can't take a number two."

"How many days has it been since the last time?"

"Speak up a bit."

"How many days has it been since you had a bowel movement?" I yelled out on the terrace. A lady was going past down on the road carrying her little granddaughter. She flinched when I yelled.

"I haven't gone poo for two days. This morning I went for a walk, now I'm going for bathing, I'm afraid of bathing."

"Why are you afraid of bathing?" I yelled.

"Because it hurts."

"Mom," the lady with her granddaughter quickened her pace, "you have to go poo, do you hear me? You have to go poo so you don't get bowel obstruction."

The veins on my neck hurt. Was my mouth so dry from all the yelling or from the Rytmonorm? I couldn't get out another word.

"Everything hurts. Everything."

I hung up.

21

"Hello?" I said eighteen or twenty years ago. "Hello? It's me."

Not for the life of me would I have said "Dad" to him, not for the life of me.

"What do you want?"

"She's here at my place. She needs five hundred marks a month to cover her costs. Give her the Croatian pension, and I'll make up the rest."

My voice was firm but not icy, I didn't want him to hear how much all this hurt me and threw me into worry and panic. I wanted to conceal from him that I was poor and didn't know how I'd make ends meet, and not for the fricking life of me would I admit to him that I was only surviving thanks to the money he'd given me several months earlier when he got seventy thousand marks from the Italians. He gave me ten. And my sister ten. War was in the air when I got that money, so I paid for new porcelain veneers for my teeth. If my husband, Tiny, and I had to flee abroad I'd have presentable jaws—who's going to employ a gap-toothed servant? I thanked him, but I never mentioned the details, what I'm telling you now. Back then, ten thousand marks was like a million to me. I calmly waited for the carnage to begin, certain that my husband, Tiny, and I would survive because money can buy everything: medicines, food, escaping the beleaguered country, and peace of mind.

I used to go to my old hometown once a week to pick up stock. Every time I'd tell myself I wasn't going to sneak into that hotel anymore, I wasn't going to look at my father through the one-way glass, and I wasn't going to get agitated if I looked at him because it wasn't good for my health. The old man was so helpless that I could easily have pushed him off his wooden chair and stepped on his head if I wanted to. I'd park next to Aunt Katica's house, go back to the square, enter the hotel, and head into the bar to the right of the reception desk. It was usually empty because the coffee was worse than in the Bar and twice as expensive. I'd look furtively at my father through the big window, from behind the pillar, although there was no way he could see me. An ordinary old man. A fisherman. Gaunt. Sitting. A stick, wide trousers, a colorful flannel shirt, a thin neck, a seamed and haggard face, sunglasses, and thinning, gray hair. Gnarled hands on the metal table. In front of him a small glass of white wine. The frail old man would soon have to pay someone to carry him to the front door of the shack where he lived. My hands trembled, my palms were clammy, my heart fluttered, and my stomach cramped up. I looked at the half-dead old man and sweated. As if it was just yesterday that Mom sent me with Dad to take food to Nika the dog.

The house would be full of the stench when Mom made food for Nika. The big casserole most often contained the lungs of some animal cooked up with bread. He waited in his room. She'd call him as soon as the mixture cooled down. She'd hand him the casserole in a cloth bag and say to me: "Go with your dad." And I did. Summertime. He held the bag in his left hand, and I walked on his right. We went via the square, along the beach, past the monument, then the house surrounded by a sea of pebbles that has been bought by that Russian, and on beside the sea. Him on the left, me on the right. We never touched. The locals would greet us, and we greeted them back. He'd only grab my hand on the steps that led to the cage where fierce Nika was waiting. She didn't like him. He'd put on thick leather gloves that he kept in the little concrete house separated from the cage by a wall. He cautiously opened the door of the cage, emptied the stinking contents of the casserole into the feeding trough, and quickly closed the iron door again. Then we'd go into the little concrete house, first me, then him. He'd lean me against the wall and I'd look out at the pines through the little window. He'd bend over a little, press himself up to me, and rub himself against me; he rubbed and rubbed, and ground against me until finally he shuddered. The smell of garlic and white wine was in my nose. Not once, not one single time, did I say to him: "Don't, Dad." I didn't cry. We'd leave the little house, Nika always howled, and we'd go down the steps and back. Beside the sea, past the house that was bought by the Russian, then the monument, along the large beach, the square, and up the stairs into the house where we lived. He'd take the casserole down to the basement and then go to the Bar for a drink. I'd sit in the corner of the kitchen and look at Mom. She'd look back at me but she never saw me.

We were at her bedside: Tiny, my husband, and I. When we entered the room, Tiny went straight up to her, hugged and kissed her. She smiled with thin, white lips.

"You've all come—why is that? Is it my birthday today?"

"Thank God you're in a bit better mood."

"Last night they gave me two tablets, and this morning one. I yelled and screamed. They told me that worried people were gathering at the window, and still I screamed."

"Mom, for God's sake, you're not in your right mind . . ."

She looked at me with her left eye. Her right eye was swollen and closed. "You don't believe me."

"I believe you," my husband said. "Go on and scream if you're feeling bad, they're paid to help you."

"Here, Mom, I'll comb your hair a bit."

"Raise my bed."

I picked up the remote.

"No, let Tiny do it, you don't know how," she said. Tiny took the remote and gently raised the head of the bed. "See? And when you do it, it makes my back crack."

Tiny ran the comb through her gray fluff and sniffed at it. "Nana, they've washed your hair."

"Yesterday was bathing, two of them held me, I yelled and screamed, bathing hurts the most."

"When are you going to get over those diapers?" I asked.

Her eye filled with water.

Tiny stroked her head. "Nana, Mom's bad, just you poop the way you want."

A nursing attendant came in with a bowl of Chocolino crispies in warm milk. "Granny, are we going to have din-din now or when your visitors have gone? Maybe better now while it's warm?" She put a napkin around her neck and fed her with a big spoon. My mother swallowed and swallowed so as not to choke. "Attagirl," said the nursing attendant and went around her mouth with the spoon, and then with the napkin. "Well done, Granny. See, you can when you want to," she patted her on the face, turned toward us, and smiled from ear to ear.

"Lower my bed," my mother said, "cover me up."

Tiny tucked her in.

"Turn me on my side, no, on the right. I feel sick, I'm going to die soon."

"Mom, what the heck!" I screamed. "Cut it out with that dying!"

Tiny and my husband both looked at me.

"Calm down, Mom."

"The lady is fine, she sleeps like a log at night, but look at me, my legs are two posts, you can touch them, if the nurses didn't turn me every two hours, day and night, bedsores would eat me away."

The Immobile Lady in the corner eyed us with concern.

22

I WANTED TO name the shop Angelus.

Ana disagreed. "You haven't seen it, but just near here on the road into town there's a butcher's shop called Angelus. Babe, once I found maggots in their mince . . ."

"We need to find some way of telling people that we sell guardian angels." I glanced at Pino, who was painting an angel's hair red.

"Why not call the shop Guardian Angels? What do you think, gals?"

We laughed heartily. "Pino, you're a sweetheart, a pure genius," I said.

"You'll even fall in love with me when my legs grow back."

"You already have a woman who loves you. Two would be too much for you."

Pino had a wife, a sturdy woman who carried him up the stairs into the workshop every morning. Several times a day she brought him food and took the cigarette out of his mouth. I've already mentioned that none of us were interested in making big dough. Guardian Angels could have been the city's most successful firm if I were more ambitious. I could enter an agreement with the Chinese. Perhaps you didn't know that the Chinese supply coarse salt to the best-known Croatian saltworks, where it's ground and sold to us as locally produced salt. Whoever does business with the Chinese can't fail. I didn't want *Made in China* in my shop, at least not Chinese products alone.

When I sold my mother's house, we bought the one we live in now. We have a new Audi A8, and I pay for my mother's place in the home where the richest Croatian woman's own mother lives. My husband enjoys his work. He doesn't want a bar of his own because then we wouldn't be able to travel. If I had a gigantic firm . . .

When I got that idea, I talked with a doctor friend. I didn't tell him the details but just asked him for a piece of advice, and he told me: "Medicine is so very expensive these days, my dear. If you go into business in a big way, who knows if you'll earn as much as you need to treat the illnesses you wouldn't have got if you hadn't gone into business in a big way." That tipped the scales, and today I'm glad.

Which angels sell best? It's hard to say, really. The big, life-size ones of solid wood are bought by people who have the means. Five hundred euros is a lot of money.

And still, not a day passes without us selling a chubby cherub. I had an argument with Pino once because customers would always look for a little penis between the chubby little legs and were very disappointed when they didn't find it. Pino was unyielding. "Angels are asexual and incorporeal beings, real angels are actually just light, each of us has a guardian angel but it only takes on physical form when we're in big trouble, angels normally don't have a body." He found all that on the internet. He worried me.

"Pino, if angels only have a body when people are in distress our business will fail. Then buying a wooden angel would really mean buying a problem. Who'll come into the shop?"

"Don't worry, we all know what the dwarfs do with Snow White, and people still keep them in their gardens. You can tell people if they really ask—but they won't—that it's better to have a wooden angel in the house than a plaster rapist out front."

"Hello? Hello? Hello?"

Her voice was strangely squeaky.

"Hello? Hello? Hello?"

I hung up.

My cell phone rang. I didn't answer.

23

"It's a message from her, not me," I told him twenty or so years ago. "You have two pensions. Give her the Croatian one or she'll sell the house you live in. I have nothing to do with this, I'm just the messenger. Think about it. Have a good think."

My father puffed and blew into the phone. I could tell he was restless and unsettled, but in no way frightened, angry, or abusive. "All right," he said, "all right, we'll see."

We both hung up. We'll see. Who? Who'll come out on top, who is the enemy, what are we at war about? We're at war about my mother's right to freedom. My mother had moved out and was now looking back at the cage from the outside. I had also left.

"I called this morning, but you were asleep."

"Hello? Hello? Yes, who is it?" Her voice was unusually expressionless.

"It's me. How are you?"

"Tell Tiny to bring a check for me to sign, I'm going to die soon, don't forfeit the money, the Italians are sending a double pension this month, you mustn't forfeit the money . . ."

"Mom, are you ever going to stop it? You're not going to die!" I yelled into the receiver. "The doctors have examined you—you're healthy. A healthy but depressive woman. You'll outlive all of us."

"Lucky you," she said. "Did you give my Rabby some parsley?"

I hung up. My hands were shaking.

24

"You cunt," he said, although otherwise he never swore, "not you or that bitch will blackmail me. I'm not giving her a single cent. Just remember what your mother was like when you were a child. I worked all my life. I dug, I fished, I planted flowers, I chopped wood, all so that you got an education, but she could sleep till ten. If it weren't for your grandma, you wouldn't have made it to your first birthday. You would have died of hunger. If I wasn't good to her, why didn't she leave before? If I wasn't good to you, why didn't you complain? You never said no. I didn't force you to do anything. I only walloped you when you were small. Everything was fine for you and her, for years. But then you left, and now her as well. Why did you leave? All of a sudden, overnight? In the morning you didn't say a thing. Did you ever? Did you complain at all, you cunt?"

"Fuck you," I said to my father.

I hung up before he did.

"This pain is unbearable, why don't they give me something? I beg you, please ask them why they're not giving me anything?"

I said to her: "They're going to stick a patch on you, be patient!"

"It doesn't help, it doesn't help at all."

I turned to my husband and said: "Again, 'it hurts so bad, so bad, so bad.' What a put-on," I laughed.

My husband laughed too. To gratify me.

25

I USED TO think, and I still do today, that my mother had a right to freedom. But why did I have to resolve all the technical details for her? True, she was a weak little woman who was never able to take her life into her own hands. But on the other hand, aren't moms—weak little women—entitled to seek assistance from their daughters? What debt am I returning my mom?

She'd often say: "If I hadn't had you, if I hadn't needed to breastfeed you, if my mother hadn't forced me to get married, if she hadn't made me quit my job, I'd be a human being today. You've sucked all the good out of me—you, your sister, your father, my mother, and my brother. You've devoured me." She'd look me straight in the eyes as she said that, gaunt, trembly, unkempt, and nervous, with a half-smoked cigarette in her hand.

I never replied: "Fuck you! I didn't ask you to have me. Why didn't you have an abortion, isn't abortion the great discovery of modern medicine? If you'd wanted to, if you'd only wanted to, you could have dumped my grandma and my father and my sister and me. Who was stopping you? Where does it say that a married woman with children has to sleep in the same bed as her mother, to be there for her in case her migraine sets in, or she vomits, or just belches? Remember Aunt Anica, who left two children and a husband and went to Germany, and she never called or came back again. And all the breastfeeding . . . Why did you breastfeed me when you could have given me cow's milk, you trembly old cow!"

Trembly old cow?! Was my mother really a helpless thing like that? What does a trembly cow look like? And why a cow? Cows seem dim-witted, but I've never seen a nervous cow. They're gigantic, calm, placid creatures, except when a fly gets in their eye. A glance at their big, full udders always calms me. No, my mother was never a cow. She didn't relax or calm me. Whenever I looked at her, I'd tense up and feel awkward. And then guilty. Why do I, why do I alone in the world not like my mom? Where is my real mom?

The phone rang, rang, and rang. Tiny had promised to go and see her, so I didn't pick up the receiver. My cell phone was off.

26

It was me who sold our first golden angel against swine flu. Pavica was away; she has some issue with her lungs and the specialists at the Jordanovac Clinic in Zagreb are the best in Croatia, you just have to be able to get an appointment. A lady my age came into the shop; I'm telling you this so you'll see it's not always easy to make good money. She was sniffing and her eyes were red from crying.

"Hello," I smiled from ear to ear, "I hope you haven't got swine flu." My cell phone vibrated but I didn't answer it. I never answered my mother's calls during working hours.

The woman wiped her eyes with the palm of her hand. "I haven't got swine flu. I'm crying, but I just have glaucoma."

"I'm glad you don't have swine flu, it hasn't reached our city yet, though I hear it could break out any day, God only knows how much we can believe in vaccination, some claim it kills more than it helps, the pharmaceutical industry has been accused of genocide, and an Austrian journalist has charged some Americans and other crooks of poisoning us with their vaccines . . ." I gave her another big smile, holding a golden angel in my hand.

The woman looked at me. "No, I just have glaucoma."

"How awful," I said. "You have to drink a lot of tea and take care of yourself, but in this time of swine flu we can also offer you . . ."

"My husband told me I go out too much, that I was always on the road, that my eyes were funny, so I must be out looking for a lay. I have three grandchildren, I go to the market to buy vegetables—I don't deserve comments like that."

I was amazed. The lady was my age, like I said, and very neglected. She had a dark growth, and tufts of pale hair grew up out of her head like desert grass. Her eyes were red, her face was pale, and water dripped from her nose into a tissue.

"How awful. If you need protection we have a wide range here," I said.

I put the golden angel back on its shelf and took down a Denver-blue one that protects against bad moods.

The lady wiped her nose: "You have to admit, it's totally inappropriate to say something like that to a woman like me who has trouble both with her back and with her eyes. Imagine, 'You're out looking for a lay.' I went to see an ophthalmologist. First, he thought I had glaucoma, that's why my eyes are red, and it's true that the ocular pressure is up in the left eye, but only slightly, so he thought it was an allergy, and he gave me some drops that raised my blood pressure significantly, so I gave up the therapy. I always wear glasses with photosensitive lenses, but I took them off before I came in here. That first ophthalmologist thought I had glaucoma, so then I went to see a private specialist, and he told me I really do have glaucoma. That's why I now use drops and am constantly under observation. In the ophthalmologic surgery they drip a fluid into your eyes for dilating your pupils and tell you to wait twenty minutes. But where? There are only two chairs in the ward, so you go out in front of the hospital and wait the twenty minutes. In the wintertime you ramble about the hospital and run into a lot of people, all of them ill. A lot of people say hello to you because this is a small town, but they don't know your pupils have been dilated and you're as blind as a bat, so they get offended when you don't say hello back. When they dilated my pupils the last time, I scarcely recognized my own sister in the corridor, but she didn't recognize me either because they'd dilated her pupils too, the thing with the eyes is genetic, and my father is . . ." She tried to catch her breath.

"Did your mother have problems with her eyes too?"

"I use artificial tears in my eyes because over the years you stop producing your own, that's why old people don't cry at funerals even if one of their own children is being buried. Some claim that old people don't cry because the years kill off emotions, you become more and more selfish and apprehensive, you only cry about yourself and don't give a damn even about those closest to you. I disagree. Old people aren't bad like that. If they had good children who bought them artificial tears—a small bottle costs thirty-something kuna—they'd be more compassionate, they'd show physically that they suffer, and so the children would also love them more." The lady wiped her red eyes. "I just wanted to tell you that it's not pleasant to have problems with your eyes, and then your husband says you're out looking for a lay . . . I didn't say it because I was afraid he'd slap me in the face, but I could have asked him how he'd damn well feel to be awash with artificial tears, greasy from chloramphenicol, and wet from corticosteroid? He doesn't care, and I'll tell you something else . . ."

I smiled from ear to ear again and patted her on the right shoulder: "Do please calm down. Perhaps your husband is just afraid of swine flu. We're all anxious, we're all tense and nervous because of it, and that's why people often say things they don't really mean . . ."

"You think my husband is afraid of swine flu, but he was already like that when the flus . . ."

"The latest research shows that the fear of swine flu causes terrible aggression in men. I can offer you . . . ," I said, returning the Denver angel to the shelf and taking the golden one, "protection from aggression *and* the flu. One hundred and forty-nine kuna is no big deal today."

The lady left the shop greatly calmed, with the golden angel in a paper bag.

In the next few days we'll be getting declarations that say the angels are "authentically Croatian." That will help business a lot.

"I took a number two in the toilet today. You can see I'm making an effort, but you think I'm not. It hurts so much, every bone."

"Congrats," I said. "Does that mean you can now do without diapers?"

She got offended. "There you go again, asking too much and exaggerating. Take it slow! They told me you needn't bring diapers to the home, you don't even need to pay for them, they put that on the invoice."

27

I CALLED MY father again. "It's me." I wanted to tell him that my nose had been permanently impaired by his white wine and garlic. Not true. I drink white wine when I have to, when it's someone's birthday and they insist, and when I owe them something. If I didn't, I wouldn't be with them on their birthday. I hate white wine, it gives me a sore stomach, and its odor makes me wince. Or is it that I, although well into my "mature years" (that's putting it mildly), can't stand my father in my nose? I don't like myself when I'm precious and uppity like that. Garlic, white wine, the smell of my father, the stench of my father—so what? The old man is in the ground. I cooled off long ago, so why this obsession? You also have a father and also have problems with old people. I'm not the only daughter in the world whose dad loved them too much.

And Josef Fritzl? The guy from a small Austrian town who slammed his daughter in the basement for years and made her have eight children? Or was it six? Or four? In any case, everyone's heard of him. It turned out later that there are more Fritzls in this world. The Austrian authorities plan to demolish his house because people gather in front of it. That's unfair. Fritzl's house is a monument that's just as important as any other monument in the world, whose role is to keep the memory of the victims alive. Why is the soldier killed in war a loss we must never forget, but a daughter sexually enslaved for years is condemned to oblivion? If all the houses where fathers molest their daughters were demolished, the world would look like Dresden.

I'll google Dresden. "In the night from February 13 to 14, 1945, the completely unprepared city was attacked by more than 800 British and American bombers, which dropped 1,478 tons of high-explosive bombs and 1,182 tons of incendiaries. Over 25,000 buildings and 90,000 apartments were destroyed during the attack, and 25,000 inhabitants lost their lives."

Fritzl is a monster? You don't know one single father who fucks his daughter? Recently I was out for dinner and we talked about Fritzl. All of us around the table were horrified, we're civilized people. Some said that sort of thing could only happen in a perverse country like Austria, which looks like a picture book on the outside, but inside there are Fritzls and Jörg Heiders.

Then one of the men—I don't know him—said it wasn't fair to talk like that about the Austrians. He lives on the island we could all see from the restaurant terrace: "For example, there's a father on my island who fucks his daughter. Everybody knows it except her mom."

We were disgusted.

"Why doesn't anybody report him to the police?" My husband hates violence.

"Who? Nobody wants to get mixed up in it."

My friend Kika said: "Why couldn't you tell her mom or write her an anonymous letter? She might be able to help."

"Her mom? Are you crazy? She couldn't care less. Even when it's revealed that a dad has been raping his little girl for years, nobody ever asks where her mom was. Forget her mom." That was my voice.

My father rejected my suggestion. He changed his mind overnight. No, he wasn't agreeing, he wouldn't move out of her house into his place by the sea. His little house was old and damp, and he had neither the strength nor the will nor the money for renovations, he had given cash to me and my sister, he wouldn't give my mother his Croatian pension, so she had to pay for her choice herself.

"You know full well . . . ," I stressed. "A little while ago you said you wouldn't move out, so you know full well that the house you're living in isn't yours. You know full well that the house you're living in is hers. And you know full damn well that I'm flesh of your flesh and blood of your blood."

I thought up the bit about the flesh and blood, and perhaps I didn't say "you know full well" quite so many times, I don't like to have to emphasize what I say. I told him we were similar, and added: "I'll sell the house with you in it."

I sold the house with him in it.

"How are you today?"

"I dreamed the same dream again."

"What did you dream, Mom?" I held the phone in my hand and watched a ginger cat on the terrace.

"I dreamed my mom was pulling my hair. She pulled my hair all night, and I cried."

"Mom . . . ," the cat was observing the little red birdhouse and waiting for another bird to come down and land, "it must be a good feeling to wake up from such a terrible dream and realize that your mom is gone."

"I can't hear you, speak up a bit . . ."

"What did you have for lunch today?"

"Greens. Who's going to come? Why doesn't anybody come?"

"I'm coming tonight. What should I bring?"

"Tissues and Horse Balm."

28

I WAS BRAVE twenty years ago. Short sentences, a clear tone, the main thought as sharp as a razor. Fathers are violent and men are violent. A woman is bashed in Croatia every fifteen minutes. The ratio of men and women who kill each other in relationships is one to a hundred, perhaps even one to a thousand. I want to say that a woman knows how to talk with her odious man properly when she's certain he's far enough away. If her mom's on the other end of the line . . .

"I'm in terrible, terrible pain. I ate everything, yogurt too, I didn't go to the restaurant because I'm in terrible pain, but I made it to the door of the restaurant, a fine lady walked me. When I sat down at the table, I felt a stab of pain, I screamed, two ladies brought me back to bed, my bones hurt so much."

If my mother went to the restaurant independently, I'd pay a thousand kuna a month less.

29

HIS PANTING. HIS quivering voice in the receiver: pleading, plaintive, old, and frail.

"Is that you?"

"It's me."

He cried. He whimpered. He whined. That was my father twenty years ago. I'd waited for that moment all my life: when he'd weep and whine, crawl before me in misery, plead and beg, trembling, and I'd boot him in the face, crush his head under my heel, gouge out an eye with the tip of my shoe, kick him in the balls, send a rig with a trailer to run over him . . .

It didn't look like that at all. I thought I was going to be sick, the palms of my hands were clammy, I felt awkward and uncomfortable as if *people* were watching me, although I was in the living room by myself, I wanted to hang up and return the money to the new owner of the house.

"I'll give you the pension, I'll give you five hundred marks a month, I'll give it for a year in advance, I'm a poor old man, what can I do, where can I go, why . . ." He called me by my name, not my real name but what he used to call me when I was a little girl; he didn't use that name or any other when I grew up. He also said "my daughter, my daughter," into the phone to me that day.

I told him in an icy voice, doing my very best, and calling to mind those pictures: "You obviously don't know me, you have no idea who I am. When I said I'd sell the house, I was telling you that I'd sell the house, nothing more or less than that. Where did you get the idea I was joking, that I was being frivolous? If you have a suggestion or an idea, if you want to spend a short time longer in that house, you can call your new master."

I hung up. Laid down on the couch. Closed my eyes.

"Today I did a number two in the toilet and went for a walk with the therapist, I walked and walked."

"Mom, but today is Sunday, the therapists don't work on Sundays."

"But I thought today was Monday."

30

Aw, MY HEART really bleeds for you. Get the fuck out of there, old man, who gives a damn? I've sold the house, now get your ass into gear . . . And fuck you, Mommy dearest. Ditch those diapers or I'm gonna send you headfirst into the next dumpster! Stop playacting as if everything hurts when the doctors say you're not in pain.

"She's not in pain, not in the slightest. We watch her from the corridor, and her face is completely relaxed when she thinks no one's watching, but as soon as anyone comes near she starts to whine and scream. She isn't all cramped up in pain, don't be taken in. Old people can be excellent playactors."

"You know, she sleeps all night, she breathes calmly the whole night long. I can't get a wink of sleep since the operation, my legs are like two posts. I can't sleep, she's lying, she lies as soon as she wakes up, when you're here she screams and cries for help, and as soon as you're gone she gets up by herself, sits there, and drinks coffee from the vending machine through a straw."

I told her: "Tiny will come today, I've got pneumonia."

She screamed.

31

I WAS TWELVE. I wanted to go upstairs to the room my sister and I shared. Dad was in the hall. I went past him, making for the stairs. When my back was turned, he pulled me toward him and fondled my breasts, and then let me go. Mom was two yards away in the kitchen making soup. I went upstairs to the bathroom. When inside, I took a large pair of scissors, and sheared off half my hair. Then I went down into the kitchen. Mom was making soup. She turned toward me. "Set the table," she said.

Maybe my dad was the most ordinary of dads, like yours, and it was just me who was unusual?

I lay there coughing. My husband made me tea and brought it to me in bed.

"Plus, you've got a double bunch of Peruvian lilies, salt-free curd cheese from Pag, Lindt milk chocolate with hazelnuts, *The Sound of the Sixties* as a five-CD set, and, since you like popular psychology, *The Web of Life* by Mirjana Krizmanić."

"What did I do to deserve such kindness? How is she?"

"She had a coffee with chocolate, didn't complain about being in pain, and her brother belted her all night."

"Did she have her teeth in?"

"I didn't look. She said to say hello and hopes you get better soon. She asked when Tiny was going to come. I called Tiny and told her I was up there and she needn't come today, so she'll go to see her tomorrow, don't worry. Here, drink this, it's French herbal tea, without theine, not too hot, not too cold."

"Is she still in diapers?"

"You ask me too much."

32

My mother never hit me. Never. I wouldn't hear the crack of some primeval whip when I talked with her. And yet I usually kept clear of her. I regret that I don't know how my mom smelled, I've always felt so guilty because I've looked on her as if she was *your* mother, not my own. I didn't stroke her gray hair, but I should have, and I would have if she wasn't my mother. I didn't pat her white, bony shoulder, and I would have if she wasn't my mother. I didn't look into her bleary eyes, and I would have if she wasn't my mother . . . How can you talk with a mother you don't love? There's a mass of literature about malicious fathers, and women are always the victims, but I can't handle communication with my mother. She was a victim because she lived with my father, she was a victim because she was born to my grandma and thrashed by her late brother when she was small, and she was a victim because I was her daughter. Who am I? What am I?

I recently watched a TV documentary about a terribly fat young man who weighed almost seven hundred pounds and had a mean father. "I became such a sad thing because of my dad," he said.

The fat man's mom smiled as he spoke those words. His dad had beat him, his brother, their sister, and their mother. She'd always been with her little children and her husband, whom death had since taken from her.

"I loved him," the lady said.

"I never loved him," my mom said. "Bring me tissues, a comb, cold cream, and iced tea—not in a big bottle, in a small one. I didn't go to the restaurant or the toilet, everything hurts, I didn't get a wink of sleep last night, they'll give me something today so I can go poo in my diaper."

33

I was reading a book. I must have been seven years old. Father came in and snatched the book from my hands, our tomcat Lynxy scooted from my lap. My mother looked on dully, moved away from the table, and went upstairs. My father bashed me on the head with the book. He looked at me from up close, an ogre of white wine and garlic. And anger to vent.

"You read, read, read. Why don't you *do* something? Why are you always reading? What will ever become of you?"

A lock of my hair was in his fist. I stood, watched, and waited. My father, disgusted, wiped his hand on his pants, and my hair fell to the floor. He proceeded to turn the book into little pieces of paper. "There, go and wash the dishes and help your mom, you lazy cow!"

That's a sad story because there was no "yellow phone" in Croatia fifty-three years ago. Even if there had been such an emergency number, it wouldn't have been any use to me because we didn't have a telephone at home. A yellow phone? Do children really call the yellow phone in Croatia today when their dad tears out their hair? I'll google "children, mistreatment, phone, aid . . ." It's not called "yellow phone" but "Brave Phone" in Zagreb and "SOS phone" here in my city, and children can call it until 9 p.m. But what if your horny dad starts biting your neck around 9:30? Do you have to wait until morning or thump on the bathroom door, in the hope that mom might open?

"I'm a bit better today," she said into the receiver. "How are you?"

"A bit better too."

"Look after yourself," she said.

I coughed loudly, wiped my nose, coughed again, and then hung up.

34

For years, I considered fathers who loved their daughters to be depraved. Until I had Tiny. But sometimes I still shiver when my husband hugs Tiny. She often puts her arms around his neck—around mine too, but more often around his. They laugh loudly together. I seldom laugh, I'm a serious woman. They've always been close. I think she loves him more than she does me. Who knows how her dad smells to her? Does she know how I smell? How do I smell to my daughter? My husband is the tenderest creature on earth. He's like a mom to me. Who is my mother? What's wrong with our mothers? Why do we daughters not mention them? All mothers are monuments of suffering, they gave birth to us, they fed us, they often mention breastfeeding even if they never pulled out a breast for us; I gave birth to you, I breastfed you, I-you, I-you, how twangy. Women are always coming into our shop. Not one of them has her mom in her nose. They don't say: "She looks after my kid but she'll rub it in my face forever." They don't complain: "She never liked my husband, when we separated she said, 'My daughter, who'll look after you now?'" Nor will she tell the psychiatrist: "I go to her apartment three times a day, my brother is nowhere in sight, and she keeps saying, 'My son is the only one who loves me.'" They're flabbergasted when they hear from their moms: "Your husband is a wonderful man, what did he see in you?" It isn't considered respectable to quote one's mother. My customers speak ill only of men.

A woman of my age came in on Friday. In the end, I sold her a bright-red angel. He, she, or it—experts are still debating—protects you against depression.

"My husband and I loved each other very much, we have two daughters, and then he told me last week, after I'd made him Olivier salad—no, I didn't buy frozen vegetables, I chopped all the carrots myself . . ." She mentioned some of the other ingredients too, but I've forgotten them.

"He told me . . . there was still some mayonnaise around his mouth, I really hate it when he talks with his mouth full and doesn't wipe off the mayonnaise, the damn mayonnaise, as if it's so hard to wipe your mouth with a napkin. He told me: 'This is pointless, I . . .' I interrupted him: 'Before you tell me what's pointless, please, please, please, just for me, wipe the damn mayonnaise off your damn mouth and finish chewing the Olivier before you tell me what's pointless. Is it so hard to finish your mouthful and then speak? I really wonder about your mother, the woman never worked, but she never taught you not to talk with your mouth full.' He said: 'This is pointless, I . . .' 'Listen,' I interrupted, 'please, please, just for me, wipe your mouth, you'll make me sick if you don't.' So he wiped his mouth and then said to me: 'This is pointless, I'm leaving.' 'You're leaving? Where to? Huh, where to?'"

The lady took a moist tissue out of her bag and wiped her eyelids. They were the same color as our angels that protect against depression.

"He told me: 'It doesn't matter where, I'm leaving, I can't see any point in this anymore . . .' 'No point in what, what are you talking about, just because I told you to wipe your mouth? You're a successful man, you often go to dinners with business partners, you ought to know that you have to wipe your mayonnaisy mouth, that you shouldn't talk with your mouth full, business partners . . .' 'I've never been to business dinners, I . . .' 'What?' I asked, 'What do you mean you've never been to business dinners . . .' 'Or on business trips,' he said. 'Where did you go, then?' 'That doesn't matter anymore,' he said and put a spoonful of Olivier into his mouth—with the serving spoon. He ate the Olivier straight out of the bowl although he knows that drives me up the wall. He looked me straight in the eyes. And I looked at him. Then he got a plastic container out of the cupboard, took a big scoop of salad with the serving spoon, plopped it into the container, put the lid on, and left the apartment."

"Where was your mom then?"

"My mom . . ." The woman searched for something in her large bag. She took out a packet of tissues. "My mom still doesn't know anything about it. She idolizes my husband, so I don't know how to tell her. My mom's very sensitive, I mustn't burden her with my problems. She has high cholesterol."

"Apart from having high cholesterol, how is your mom?" The lady made a nervous impression, her red eyelids trembled. "You should tell her after all, it'll make you feel better."

"No, I'll leave my mom in peace, I fear she could have a stroke. She always ordered Italian cheese for my husband, not Reggiano but Padano, or the other way round, and my husband knew which cheese my mom likes most, I just can't remember. I couldn't sleep at all that night. In the morning I took a shower, some people shower in the mornings, some in the evenings, I shower in the mornings, always in the mornings."

"Some people don't shower at all," I said with a big smile so the lady would feel a bit better.

"I got into my car, and he drove his SUV, which technically is ours, not his, we took it on lease, so actually it's neither ours nor his. Anyway, he got into it, but not into my car, which is neither his nor mine but belongs to his father. I got into the car and headed toward Trieste." She returned the packet of tissues into her large, pale-red Kenzo bag. "I didn't drive into Trieste because the meadow is right next to the Slovenian-Italian border, on the former border, a dirt road leads to the meadow, about two miles, and I drove there to the dwarf." The lady opened the Kenzo bag again. "The dwarf is still there. His colors have faded a bit, but he's still there."

"Would you like me to hop over to the bar and get you tea or coffee? You're very upset . . ."

"No, thanks, I don't drink tea and coffee. That dwarf . . . It's a long story, I'll tell it to you all the same. We women are all sisters, aren't we? It's better that I tell it all to a stranger than to my best friend, Katarina—a woman is another woman's best enemy sometimes, like a man—she'd gloat over my misfortune. I drove there to see that dwarf again. He looked at me and I looked at him. I cried. Twenty years previously we went to a shopping mall near Palmanova, in Italy, where you can buy everything you need for the garden. It was there that I first set eyes on that dwarf, there really was something special in his expression. It didn't seem dumb and cheerful like dwarfs' faces usually do, dumb and cheerful; each of them grins and has a little red cap on his head, but not this one. He looked at me and I looked at him, and I said to my husband: he's the one. He bought me that dwarf, and I didn't even let him put the dwarf in the trunk because the little fellow had such a human feel to him; he sat on the back seat. It really made me happy that my husband bought me the dwarf although I knew what he thinks about our Snow White, who still stands in the garden in front of the house. And will stay there. I'll fight for my part of the house until my final breath! I'll take a lawyer," the lady howled.

"Please calm down," I said. "Would you like me to get you a drink from the bar? Would you like some Xanax?"

She put both tablets into her mouth. "My husband turned off toward the meadow. I realized straightaway what he wanted, it was all clear to me, but, you know, I don't believe the films where he and she get undressed in the hall, in a rush, they've just climbed the stairs to the apartment, and they're so turned on that they cast off their clothes and start to bang right there in the hall, do you believe films like that?"

The lady laughed nervously. I smiled from ear to ear.

"I don't like sex if I can't have a good wash beforehand. My husband knew that, and never before had we turned off the road like that, it was the first and last time. He didn't ask me anything, and I didn't want to seem ungrateful, after the dwarf. We got undressed, and I said, 'Just a sec,' and whipped some Bi-Facil out of my handbag, it's a liquid eye-makeup remover, Lancome, the best eye-makeup remover, a dark-blue fluid, and I splashed myself a little down there, just a bit, as much as was possible in those conditions. I didn't want to use too much of it because a small bottle costs almost three hundred kuna. My husband said later: 'You're nuts!' He tried to spit out that Lancome, I got a bottle of Coke out of the car. 'Why didn't you wash yourself with Coke? You're crazy!' I never liked it when he said that to me, but there was the darling dwarf, so I passed over it. Then he said: 'I love you, I truly love you, you're my mousie, let's mark the spot here, let's leave the dwarf here where we made love, may it forever be a monument to our love.' I said: 'No way, Snow White's waiting for him, he's the first . . .' But my husband just hugged me. We were still stark naked, the Lancome stung a little, I'd be lying if I said it was terrible pain, just a slight stinging, and my husband got the dwarf out of the car and put him beneath a tall tree. I waved to him as we left. And now, when I went there to see if he was still beneath that tree . . ." The woman started to open her bag, but I offered her my packet of tissues. "Thank you. He was still standing there and looking at me, and I looked at him and cried . . . I'll never forgive myself for what happened next: I take a lot of medication for my blood pressure, all of them are basically diuretics; I looked at him and he looked at me, and I just had to pee, I couldn't hold on, so I let down my panties and peed right there in front of the dwarf, I peed on our love, I . . ." The woman was distraught.

"Why don't you tell all this to your mom? You're her child after all. Every mother . . ."

"I'd rather die than get her involved in all this. My mom's in a home. It would hurt her terribly."

"Which home is your mom in?"

"Here nearby. A fine doctor runs a small home. It's practical because it's in the city center. We tried to find a place in a public home, via some priests or other, but they demanded that Mom bequeath her house to the Church. 'Listen,' I said to the priest, 'it's a two-thousand-square-foot house, and my mom is eighty-eight, where's the logic?'" The lady wiped her nose. "But that's not all," she said.

"What do you mean?"

"Six months ago he came back to me. He turned up at the doorstep and said: 'What happened, happened. You're all there is for me.'"

"That's lovely," I said. "Why are you crying? That's just beautiful."

"This morning I met Katarina, my best friend. She told me: 'I saw Ivan a little while ago in the park. He was waiting for a dog to do its business behind a bush. I didn't see the dog, but I knew he was waiting for a dog there, I know how people look who are waiting for their dog to shit, basically he looked dully into the distance and smoked. Does Ivan still smoke? And I didn't know you have a dog, you didn't tell me anything.'"

The lady collapsed on the chair from grief and put her head between her legs.

"Please do calm down. Why did that hurt so much?"

"We don't have a dog. *She* has a dog—they're together again."

"How terrible," I said. I laid the angel against depression into one of the expensive bags we normally only use for foreign customers and saw the lady out. "This is sure to help you."

"Come on, get up, cut the playacting, you look perfect, you're pink in the face, you seem healthy to me," I laughed.

"Why are you making fun of me?" she snarled and shut her eyes. That was a sign for me to go.

The Immobile Lady whispered to me: "See my two legs? They're like two posts, touch them. I'm in pain day and night, the nurses turn me every two hours. But you are a true sufferer, you poor thing!"

35

Pino, ana, and I talked at length. Should we enhance our range or stick to angels? Ana suggested we go into business with Virgin Marys too. I wasn't sure that was a good idea. If we started producing Virgin Marys it might work, but the competition in our city is stiff. Every souvenir shop sells a Mary mounted on something, most often a horseshoe; one breastfeeds a baby, but her breasts aren't to be seen; another is overtly buxom, and there's no baby and only a crown; many are covered in a golden shawl discreetly bearing Croatian interlace, discreet but unmistakable. In a zany, totally far-out shop, which mostly sells devils of all sizes, I saw a Virgin Mary riding a broom.

Pino said: "Ana, it's no problem for me to paint a Mary if you tell me how you want it done, but bear in mind that making a Mary requires much more effort than an angel, especially if we give her a baby . . . You'll lose too much time. Our range is phenomenal, we have angels for every circumstance imaginable: in white, pink, or rose for a new baby, in black for widows; for the freaks we have an angel in striped prison gear; for patriots . . ."

"I know our range, Pino."

Pino laughed, he's always laughing. Have you ever noticed that people without arms or legs are always in a good mood? I've never asked him why he's so cheerful every day. His wife loves him, and he loves her. I've often thought about whether a man would love his wife like that if she came back from Afghanistan without legs. Would he carry her into our angel workshop every day, except on weekends, place her in her wheelchair, kiss her on the hair, and go home to their children? And what if she came back from Afghanistan to a husband and they didn't yet have children—would he want to father her children? Would I love my husband if he came back from Afghanistan without legs? I'd never let him go there in the first place! Admittedly, my husband could also lose his legs in a carnival accident, fortunately he doesn't go in for carnival, or a car wreck. A rock could fall onto his car in any old Croatian tunnel, or a balcony could drop onto his legs out on the street, everything's possible. Would I love my legless husband as much as I love him today with both legs? I swear I would. I'd even sell our beautiful house and buy him the most expensive artificial legs in the world so that his leglessness would be our little secret out on the street. I'd wash his hair, dress and undress him, but I wouldn't carry him because he weighs two hundred pounds and me just one hundred and thirty, and I'm not allowed to carry heavy loads because of my back. I saw on TV that modern prostheses are a marvel. You can even walk up and down stairs normally with them. If my husband without legs still had a dick and balls of course I'd go to bed with him, perhaps a little less often because men are sensitive to handicaps, but that would suit me. I take beta-blockers, which kill my desire for sex, but that doesn't mean in any way that I want my husband to lose his legs.

We decided not to produce Virgin Marys because, as I might have said already, I didn't feel like working more and employing more people. Everyone in Croatia is in a bad mood these days, and I don't have the strength to listen to even more sad stories. Whoever comes into our shop complains about something. To be sure, our angels wouldn't sell like they do if Croatia were a land of smiles, but sometimes when I'm smiling from ear to ear at a customer I just want them to buy an angel and go.

"I'll never take a poo in the toilet again."

"Why not?"

"Because my butt hurts when I sit on the toilet."

36

I REMEMBER WAITING for the bus after school one day in my college years. It was raining and I was alone at the stop. He came up to me from behind and put his right arm around my neck as if he wanted to strangle me. He squeezed up to me. "You didn't even shake. Anyone could come up to you from behind and they'd be welcome. Why didn't you resist?"

"Resist?" I asked and left his arm around my neck. "My own father?"

"How did you know it was me?"

"You're the only man who rubs up against me."

I didn't say anything about the wine or the garlic. Would what he did count as molestation today?

What would they ask a daughter in court if she reported a father who came up to her from behind at the bus stop? "Did you notice if the man had an erection?"

Yes, he had an erection, but that was forty-five years ago. Back then, Dad's erections were different from what they must be like today.

Would Mom be at the trial? What would the judge ask her? And what would she say?

I tried calling her. She didn't answer.

I called several times more. She didn't pick up the receiver.

The nurse said: "We've given her something, don't you worry, she's sleeping."

37

"Today I ate a whole bowl of greens. When's somebody going to come? I called you this morning. Where were you?"

"At the hairdresser's."

"That's good, if you go to the hairdresser's it means you're in a good mood."

"You can order a hairdresser too."

"Me? You don't understand a thing. How am I supposed to even go to the bathroom? Bathing hurts."

38

I went to see the head nurse.

"Your mother is recovering very well, she's slightly depressive, but she still eats five times a day, she insists on pureed food, she doesn't eat independently, she doesn't get out of bed because she doesn't want to, our nursing attendants make an effort but for now your mother refuses to go to the bathroom by herself, she doesn't want to sleep in an ordinary bed, she's afraid of falling out." The head nurse smiled from ear to ear.

"What did they tell you, how am I?"

"They told me that you're healthy, you don't need diapers, can go in an ordinary bed without wooden bars, can go to the restaurant yourself, can go to the toilet by yourself . . ."

"You're so unkind, my daughter, so unkind."

39

HER VISIT WAS quite a surprise. She came into the shop with her head covered in a colorful silk scarf. She was wearing dark glasses, her skin was grayish, her nose looked bigger on her skinny face, and her thin lips were coated in dark-red rouge. Exactly the same color as the polish on her nails, of course. She smiled. "You weren't expecting me?"

"No, I wasn't."

"They said I'd be having the chemotherapy in the afternoon, so I'm free for a few hours. I didn't know where to go and didn't feel like hanging round in the hospital cafe and chatting with 'colleagues' about who has how long left to go."

"Don't get obsessed about it. None of us has any idea how long we have left."

She sat down on the chair at the small round table next to the shop window.

"Should I hop over and get you a coffee?" The cafe terrace was just five or six yards from the window.

"No, thanks." She took a pack of cigarettes out of her green handbag.

"You're off your rocker, you're really are."

She laughed: "What are you trying to tell me, that I'll get cancer if I smoke?"

"Why don't you stop? Smoking certainly doesn't help."

She lit up a cigarette. I passed her the ashtray and opened the door.

"Smoking isn't allowed in here, the angels could catch fire and burn the shop down."

"No way. How could a shop so full of good-luck charms burn down?"

"You can have any angel you want—this one." I took a pink fatty down off the shelf. Its wings were made of colored pencils. "It brings happiness in love. If I believed in angels, I'd take this one home."

"Yesterday afternoon I was desperately trying to get to sleep, I stuck a morphine patch on my back, nothing else works, and just when I was finally dropping off to sleep he started hammering a piece of metal. The afternoon was no time for sleeping, he told me."

"Don't worry about him. When you get better everything will be different, you'll simply slam the door and leave."

"Where would I go?"

"You could work with me here, rent a small apartment, rents are lower, the financial crisis has its positive side."

"It does, everyone's looking for angels," she laughed.

"I'm glad you're cheerful."

"Yesterday I made him fried scorpion fish, the frozen variety." She had a fit of coughing.

I went into the bathroom and brought her a glass of water. I waited a few minutes for her to get over the cough, took the cigarette out of her hand, and crushed it out. "You're not going to smoke in here."

She drank the water. "You remind me of him."

"Which 'him'? Your husband or our father?"

"My husband. Once he kept me locked up in the basement for thirty days without cigarettes. I was only allowed out to piss and shit. 'You look like death warmed over,' he said."

"Who cooked for him?"

She laughed: "I don't know. A few months ago, he and I met in front of the Bar."

"Which 'he'? Father or your husband?"

"Father."

"He'd heard I was ill, and he said to me: 'You're not going in my grave.'"

"He said that to you? He really was off his rocker!"

"Good mornin', good mornin', to you," she laughed.

"What did you tell him?"

"I told him I'd never, ever make him gnocchi with prunes again. He really made my blood boil."

"Now he's six feet under a thick marble slab, praise the Lord, but he can see us."

"Yes, he can. And how's she?"

"Alive and kicking, but she keeps screaming for help: 'It hurts so bad, so bad, so bad.'"

"Playactor."

"Playactor."

"Maybe I had better luck in the separation after all," she said, getting up from the chair.

I locked the door, walked her to the main street, and kissed her yellow cheek: "I wouldn't swap with you."

"I saw your daughter," I said spitefully.

She huddled in the bed and tried to pull the lilac-colored blanket up to her neck.

"How is she?"

"She's dying."

"Really? Dying?"

"Really. Dying."

"But don't you go getting too upset. If anything happened to you . . ."

"If anything happened to me . . ." I waited.

"I ate greens and went for a walk around the institution."

"No, she didn't," whispered the Immobile Lady whose legs were like two logs. "She's lying, she's in bed all day blubbering, 'It hurts so bad, so bad, so bad . . .'"

"What's she saying, is she saying I'm bad?"

"The lady says she can't feel her legs, they're like two posts. How are you today?"

She looked at me with her blurry right eye: "Better."

"If I see her again should I say hello?"

"It's up to you."

I left the room and went to the upper exit. I got in the car and saw wet agave leaves. A lady in a pink coat was watering the rosemary with a hose.

40

If only I was a person and not a picture of misery . . . I was tired, I had a sleepless night behind me, and she called at seven thirty and said: "This morning I went poo by myself."

Why didn't I say: How about you just fucking shut up for a change?

41

"Now my elbows hurt."

"Your elbows?"

"My elbows."

42

An Armani blazer, a white T-shirt, jeans, Tod's moccasins, a Tod's bag—she looked fantastic.

"Your hair is lovely," I said to the woman who came into my shop with a cigarette in her mouth. Big dark-brown eyes and dark-brown, ironed hair. What did she need my angels for?

I offered her an ashtray.

"Thank you. Do you have an angel that will kill all sexual desire in my husband? We've been married for thirty years."

She picked up our most expensive angel: twenty-four inches

long, eight pounds of solid wood—Pino spent three days on it—with curly hair of coarse wool, a dark-red mouth, lilac-colored glass wings, green lacquered fingernails, and toenails on the little feet painted glossy black. Eight hundred euros. She put it back on the shelf.

"And this one here? Why isn't it colored?" Her short nails fondled the oldest angel in the shop, a wooden creature coated in matte lacquer. "I don't like this one, a fat Pinocchio without a nose!"

"From our starting-off phase. It's not for sale."

"That's a shame, I really ought to buy it, I feel like a fat Pinocchio."

"You're not fat."

"Five foot nine, and one hundred and fifty pounds—you don't think I'm fat?"

"Far from it, women of forty plus need to have a few pounds more, you look fantastic."

The lady with the pale face, dark-brown eyes, and dark-brown, ironed hair looked at me scornfully. "Why are you making me younger than I am? I don't have a problem with my age but with my husband. Where's an angel that will kill all passion in him?"

She lit up her cigarette, and I opened the shop door. "My dear," I smiled, "some women would pay in gold if we had angels that roused the slightest passion in married men. If your husband still loves you after thirty years of marriage, you ought to be happy."

She stubbed out the cigarette, and I emptied the ashtray into the garbage can. The lady was trembling. She lit up another.

I took it from her mouth and crushed it out. "Everything here is made of wood, you're not allowed to smoke."

"We've banged three times this week already. Do you think that's normal?"

I said nothing and smiled from ear to ear.

"He told me he has the right to enjoy life's pleasures. His main pleasure in life is spreading my legs, regardless of what I think about it. Where are my human rights? Who am I? Or am I a plaything like this ugly angel of yours?" She picked up the angel from our first collection. "What am I, a chunk of wood that has to spread its legs whenever the master desires?" She spread the little angel's legs.

Our latest angels can't spread their legs anymore. It increases the cost of production terribly, so we stopped. No one complained.

"Where are my human rights? Why can't I have sex just once a year if it suits me? Where's my right to go down the road yelling, 'Guys, you don't interest me anymore, hallelujah, hallelujah!'? Why do we married women have to fuck our husbands until death?"

"Calm down," I said and closed the door. "If it's too much of a strain with your husband, you can separate."

"Why should I? I love my husband, he's a wonderful man. Successful, clean, he washes every day, which most men don't, when you go into the bathroom after him you don't need a gas mask, he changes his underwear every day, we always eat out—I love him. What also exasperates me is that he reads to me in bed every evening. Without him I'd never have heard of Hemingway or Miroslav Krleža . . ."

I touched her on the shoulder. "Do you like Krleža?"

"No."

"Then why does he read you Krleža in bed?"

"That's what I'm telling you: he does whatever he wants, he fucks me whenever he feels like it, and he reads Krleža at the top of his voice. The only bit of Krleža I remember is where one of his heroes in some drama, essay, or poem says: 'Wash your hands before meals and after every emptying of the bowels.'"

I laughed. "I have no idea what Krleža wrote, my husband doesn't read, he watches ice hockey on TV, the Russian professional league, via satellite. Once only Russians played Russian hockey, they were amateurs, and the best went to America and Canada for the big money, but today there's big money in the Russian hockey league and not only Russians play there but also Czechs, Finns, and Swedes, my husband thinks that's amazing."

The lady looked at me: "I don't like sports and I don't know what you're talking about, but I don't like Krleža and I don't like sex. I don't like it. Nope, I dun laik it, as Đorđe Balašević sings in his song "Ne volem!"—I dun laik it. But I like Balašević."

"I don't like Balašević, in fact I dislike him with a passion: I dun laik 'im."

"I don't like Ambrose Bierce or his *Devil's Dictionary.*

"'*HATCHET, a young axe, known among Indians as a Thomashawk. 'O bury the hatchet, irascible Red, / For peace is a blessing,' the*

White Man said. / The savage concurred, and that weapon interred, / With imposing rites, in the White Man's head.'"

She stared at me. "You have a good memory, not in a hundred years could I learn that ditty by heart. Do you know who Alex Ovechkin and Jarome Iginla are? Márian Gáborík, the twins Henrik and Daniel Sedin, Ilya Bryzgalov, Jaromír Jágr, Vyacheslav Kozlov, and Alexander Radulov?"

"I guess they could be ice hockey players."

"You guess right."

"And do you know who said: 'He sprinkled his head with the ashes of his victims,' 'It's hardest to set fire to hell,' and 'If only one could be born after the death of one's enemy'? Jerzy Lec."

"The Russians won the final of the World Championship in 2009, I think against Canada."

"Mark Twain said: 'I don't know anything that mars good literature so completely as too much truth.'"

"Ćiro Blažević is about seventy-five and still a successful soccer trainer."

"Oscar Wilde said: 'The history of women is the history of the worst form of tyranny the world has ever known. The tyranny of the weak over the strong. It is the only tyranny that lasts.'"

"Have you ever heard of snooker? It's only shown on Eurosport, my husband roots for Ronnie O'Sullivan, nicknamed 'The Rocket.' Junhui Ding, John Higgins, Marco Fu, and Mark Allen are also good players. You wouldn't credit it, but the British and the Chinese play snooker best."

"The satirist Predrag Lucić declaimed: 'You gave me my freedom / But tore my life apart / What can I do but tell you / Thank you with all my heart.'"

"Dudu, is the greatest Croat."

"You know what Christopher S. Hyatt said . . ."

"I don't speak English."

"He wrote: 'Some think that to sell books one must be kind and let the reader off the hook. This in my mind is an insult, for the reader deserves to stay on the hook, if he hopes to do more than masturbate.'"

"I see." She grasped the lilac-colored angel in her trembling hand.

I was worried. What if it fell and its glass wings broke? Pino had a hell of a time fitting them into the wood. He gets ten percent of every expensive angel sold.

"Where's your mom?" I asked.

"My mom? What's she got to do with this? What makes you think of my mom?"

I looked at her and smiled from ear to ear.

"My mom? She died. Her theory was that a woman has to be obliging to each and every man, otherwise they'll leave her and she'll die of sorrow. No one has ever left me. It was always me who left my men. But I was obliging to them while they were with me. And that upsets me no end. Why can't we talk with them openly? Like man-to-man? I'm sick of acting, I've had enough of it all." She leveled the angel at me. "You know, you've helped me in a way. I'll go home this evening and tell him—I won't yell—I'll tell him in a normal voice: 'Old man, I haven't got a headache. It's not the atenolol, which kills all sexual desire and causes prostate cancer in men.' I've been taking it for ten years, and fortunately it hasn't made a single hair fall out. 'Old man, I haven't got an attack of high blood pressure. I simply don't feel like fucking you. Don't take it personally, I love you, I'm mad about you, I just don't feel like fucking you, goddamn it!'"

"Please do calm down," I tried to take the angel from her hand.

"Stop, stop. I'm buying it."

"Let me wrap it for you and put it in a bag."

"No need."

"Cash or card?"

"Cash."

"There's a ten percent discount when you pay cash."

She dropped it into her bag, paid, and left.

"Mom, you're becoming too strenuous for everyone. Yes, you're a strain on everyone. Just relax a bit and enjoy life! So many people your age are rotting away in holes with horrific wounds. But you have a roof over your head, heating, air-conditioning, servants, nurses, attendants, physiotherapists, doctors, a psychiatrist, Prozac . . . What do you want from life?"

"Death. Why are you yelling?"

43

"This morning I pooped twice, though it's not something I usually do."

"Bravo, Mom!"

44

"I've had enough of it all, I want to die, bring me baby lotion, a big container. Thirty-seven kuna."

45

"If I was an animal you'd club me to death or shoot me. Why am I not an animal?"

46

"A new dress again? You never had any taste. Your sister was a beauty, even in rags. This one doesn't help you either. When are you going to accept your age? Everything hurts. Why doesn't death come for me? I couldn't pass stool this morning although I ate yogurt, you didn't call me last night, shut the window, it's cold."

47

I was fifteen when my father and I went on an excursion boat to the island of Rab. She said: "You should go, Rab is lovely, you'll like it, and bring back a turtle for Grandma." She was in a brightly colored, sleeveless dress and running a broad comb through her shaggy hair. I was tall and slim and had big breasts already. A band played on the boat, and Maja Papandopulo sang. She had a beautiful voice like silver, it really rang. The drunken vacationers heard it, or maybe they didn't, as they laughed and waved to the gulls. Maja Papandopulo is no longer with us. We danced. We went up to the bridge and he introduced me to the captain. When I look at the photographs from that excursion today—the only ones where he and I are embracing—I always ask myself if that older man and that young woman are father and daughter. Is *that* my father? A destitute gardener, poor fisherman, and day laborer, human refuse incapable of getting by without bloody, grinding drudgery. An uneducated pauper from the north Croatian coast, a place on earth where all women are considered sluts except for the occasional nun. And he, of all people, had two daughters. I hated his stench, life in that hole, and his vehement contempt for money and power. Some wish to conquer the world, to become presidents of their country or at least the tenants' council. My father was devoid of ambition. White wine, little fried squid, two daughters, and a wife. That was the sum total of his life's pleasures. I never asked my sister what he did to her. Once he said to her: "You're too fat, look at your sister." She stopped eating at the age of twelve, and all her life she had the weight of a girl. Five foot four, and less than a hundred pounds. Instead of food she devoured cigarettes. If my mom had left, if she'd been a woman with guts, I wouldn't see every man as a pig, and I'd have run into a pig. I'd have married him, and today I'd go out to dinner and away for weekends with female friends my age and rehash anecdotes from my life with that pig. *He doesn't wash, doesn't cut his toenails, is afraid of the dentist, farts in his sleep and awake, boozes, has a lover but doesn't get any, so he comes home mad, with a raging erection* . . . If my mom had been better, my dad would have been mellower, and I'd live, like you, just waiting for him to kick the bucket.

My husband held my hand as we sat in the car in the parking lot of the home.

"If you can't go in, if it's too much for you tonight, don't force yourself, I'll do it."

I stayed in the car, feeling I'd betrayed her. I was so close to her, but my stomach wouldn't let me go any closer. It's not fair, it's not fair, my mother isn't my mom, she's just a sick old woman, it's not fair.

"How is she?" I asked twenty minutes later.

"Excellent, really excellent, she says to say hello. I told her you were at the dentist's."

I caressed his hand on the gearshift: "What would I do without you?"

48

He led me into the lounge. All the other passengers were outside, dancing or feeding the gulls. He undid my scarf and took it off my head. He caressed my breasts. And that was all. Am I overly sensitive? Why do I hate that dead, silent old man at the metal table? He didn't rape me, I didn't bleed between the legs, he didn't kill my lust for life, my husband is everything he isn't, the experience with my father didn't make me a person with special requirements. I have no trouble reaching orgasm, when my husband touches my breasts I don't think of my father, not even when he puts his hand between my legs. We were often in the very same bed as my mom. Quite often, in fact. My husband doesn't know. What kind of love is it between a father and his daughter? Hundreds of thousands of fathers are raping their daughters in every single part of the world right now, or at least manhandling them, licking their necks, or fondling their asses. Is that love? What is fatherly love in regard to daughters? Raping or beating them? Or at least wanting to? If it isn't talked about, does that mean it doesn't happen? My thoughts returned to Fritzl. I simply can't remember how many children he had with his daughter. I'll google him.

"Fritzl fathered four children with his own daughter. One of them died, while the others were born with serious physical deformities. He beat his own wife and children."

At the trial he was offered psychological assistance when he had to listen to the testimony of his unhappy daughter, whom he had confined, raped, and impregnated multiple times. *He* needed assistance?! Where, oh where, was his wife all those years—the mother of the raped daughter and the grandmother of those children? Where was that woman while Fritzl was away on a cruise? Who took food to old Fritzl's imprisoned lover, daughter, and the mother of his children while he was touring the Caribbean? Where, oh where, all around the world, are the mothers while the fathers are raping their daughters in the parental double bed? Dusting the living room? Cleaning the toilet? Cooking dinner? Are they silent because they're afraid? What are they afraid of? That their husbands—the fathers and rapers of their daughters—might kill them? Who told the wives of those husbands—the mothers of those daughters—that death is worse than what's happening to their daughters? When a father rapes or thrashes his daughter, he sends a message to his granddaughters and great-granddaughters too: all men are rapists and prone to violence, it's normal. Women, that's your destiny. It really is normal, it really is our destiny. But we're frustrated because men, the masters of the world and of our lives, sell us the story that it *isn't* normal and *isn't* our destiny. We only need to call social workers or the police, or tell mom. Mom? Which mom? Where's mom? Mom's cooking, washing, ironing, or reading, while he bones us. Who is mom? Mom's just a beaten-up, raped woman. She can't help us. And why would she? I'm trying to comprehend the world now at the age of sixty. Do I love my mother or am I just afraid of what *people* will say? Is that why I save her from dumpster diving?

"It hurts so bad, so bad, so bad . . . Yesterday I went poo three times."

49

WHEN I WENT into the kitchen, my mom was breading anchovies. The large frying pan was on the stove. She hadn't yet poured in the oil she used for frying fish. She kept it in a separate bottle. Back in those days, oil wasn't thrown away after just one use. Summertime. I had enrolled in teacher training and looked forward to leaving for the city. I had received a student loan and a place in a student residence. In three years' time I'd be a teacher.

"He's in the room, take him the newspaper."

"Why don't you take it?"

"My hands are messy."

I was in a thin dress. I took the kitchen rag from my mother's shoulder and rubbed it in fish blood and flour. I wrapped it around my waist and tied a knot behind my back. I took the newspaper and went into the room. He was lying on the bed in white underpants and a white tank top. A fat man in the worst years. Me eighteen, him forty-eight. Voices of people going down the stairs to the quay came in through the blinds. Stuffy semidarkness. His bed, cupboard, night table, and TV were in that room. I laid the paper by his legs. Slowly he lifted himself up. He gently drew me to him and tossed me onto the bed. He removed the stinking rag from my dress and lay on me with all his weight. How long did his panting last? Then his shuddering, wheezing, and the final gasp? Three minutes? Thirty minutes? Three hundred minutes? I didn't hear anything except the sizzling of the fish in the frying pan. Then at one point he unglued himself from me and rolled over onto his back. He gave me a push. I started for the door. He threw the dirty rag after me. I tied it around my waist again to cover up the wet spot on my dress. I glanced at him, he was reading the newspaper. When I came out of the room, I saw my mother's back. She was standing at the stove. I went up the stairs to the toilet. I didn't vomit, tremble, or cry. I left the house early that evening. I stayed for a while in Opatija with my best friend, Ema, who has since died. She found a job for me. I worked for years as a Yugotours guide. I left. My sister stayed.

"Turn me on my side."

I put my hands on her skeletal back.

"Don't touch me," she howled.

I recoiled. With my eyes, I tried to ask the Immobile Lady what was going on.

She shrugged her shoulders.

"Did you eat a bowl of greens?" I screamed.

"Why are you yelling? You're always on about food."

"You have to get your strength back."

She sneered with her toothless mouth. Her gums were almost purple.

"If all this costs you as much as they say, why don't they give me a tranquilizer or something?"

"They give you Prozac, but it takes a few weeks to . . ."

"I'm in pain today, every day, every moment. Why are you so callous? This is your revenge, I'm left to your tender mercies. Why have you never forgiven me, haven't I atoned for my sins after so many years?"

"What are you talking about?" I said into her bleary eyes.

The nursing attendant came in, a young woman in a pink dress. She was carrying a diaper. She uncovered the almost childlike body of my mother.

"See you," I yelled to my mother and went out into the corridor.

Money is a miracle. If I didn't have the dough, I'd be changing the diapers of this bony, ancient child and listening to it groan in pain. How long would I need to get used to her stench? Then again, if we were unable to pay for the doctors, for rescuing her from a heart attack, a stroke, severe anemia, and dehydration, for the operation on her anus, a detailed thyroid observation, medicine for maintaining low blood pressure, expensive creams for the care of old skin, saltwater therapy, freshwater therapy, special liquid food—if we hadn't been able to pay for all that my mother would have died at the age of sixty-five in her prime. What does modern medicine do to a person? What does modern medicine do to the children of elderly parents? It reduces them to poverty or gives them a terrible feeling of guilt. How to choose the best for old people when you don't want to give them what's best for them: their child's twenty-four-hour vigil by the sickbed?

"No way!" I said to my mother a long time ago. "There's no way I'm going to be by your side twenty-four seven."

I told my daughter: "Watch and learn, and kill me in good time."

If I wasn't a coward, I would have killed my mother long ago. For her good and mine. I would have driven her home, and she would have taken five bottles of Ultram and gone to sleep forever. But I'm a coward. The coroner would probably have noticed something, I don't watch TV, so I don't know how to kill without leaving traces, they'd do an autopsy and then put me in jail in Požega, probably for ten years. I asked my husband, and he asked the lawyers in his bar. I'd get two years, three at most. How much would that save us? In Požega I'd have free accommodation and food and feel innocent because it was a mercy killing. We pay one thousand two hundred euros per month for the home, times twelve, times three, let's make it one thousand a month so I don't have to go and get a pencil and paper; twelve thousand times three makes thirty-six thousand euros. People would kill ten others for that money in Croatia these days. The nursing attendant came out of the room, and I went back in. She smelled of the cream that's more expensive here than in the drugstore, but we pay their price because I don't want them to consider us misers. We could take our own and save sixteen kuna a month. My husband thinks that's ridiculous.

"Every kuna counts," I said.

He's practical. "We're investing in our own peace of mind, we're not throwing money away. If she'd stayed at home, we'd be paying for several carer ladies. And where would we find them? Nobody in Croatia these days would spend twenty-four hours with your mother for a thousand euros."

"For one thousand two hundred."

"Yep, one thousand two hundred."

"We're a rich country," I said to my husband sarcastically as if he was a journalist discussing the monumental laziness of the Croatian people with me.

"She slept all night, they gave her something because yesterday she was screaming all day long. I'm going to ask them to move me to another room as soon as someone dies. This is unbearable, I pay a fair price for the accommodation, and I have a right to peace. I told them to give her something, I can't go on like this." The Immobile Lady began to cry.

She was asleep.

I didn't wake her.

50

"YOU MUSTN'T BE so sensitive," the nurse in the dark-blue coat said with a big smile. "She's not in pain, she's just slowly going senile. It's always hard for the children to accept, but unfortunately we're powerless. She's in good health, but she's slowly fading. Perhaps you shouldn't come quite so often, maybe you upset her. If by chance anything happens, God forbid, we'll call you."

51

THEY WERE SLEEPING. Both she and the Immobile Lady. Her mouth was wide open.

52

DAD THE FUCKER, dad the rapist, dad the domestic tyrant, dad the war criminal, dad the killer of mother and daughter . . . Dad, dad, dad, dad. And mom? Who is mom? In every documentary about animals, I'm talking about cats, the mother cat hides her young from the father, who wants to eat or smother them so he can have a nice undisturbed fuck with the mother. I know I've already told you about that. In every documentary about big and small cats the mother moves her kittens, she looks after them, she runs with them in her teeth across the road, because she knows that the father is the enemy. Why don't we know what our father is to us? Because we're small? And does our mom, who's big, know anything about the father? She ought to. And yet she never hides us, she never grabs us by the scruff of our necks and sets off across the road. Why aren't our moms like cats when our dads are toms?

She rose from the dead. That morning she walked for twenty minutes. That's not itemized in the invoice. In the afternoon she walked for seven minutes, times two kuna per minute.

"I did a number two in the diaper because I walked too much today. You can open the window if the room stinks, the lady hasn't changed me yet."

I didn't open the window. "Mom, I've brought you the peach iced tea."

"What about the tissues?"

53

My mom? how did my mom smell when I had a dad? A sweetish odor? A sourish odor? A repulsive odor? Any odor? Do moms ever stink? No, moms don't stink. They don't stink or smell at all.

54

I didn't go up to see her. She rang three times.

Finally, I picked up the receiver. "I was at the dentist's, I have a few stitches, I can hardly talk."

"Does it hurt?" her voice trembled.

"A bit," I said.

"I'm in such pain. It hurts so much that I couldn't get a wink of sleep. Take care of yourself, my daughter."

I cried.

55

"See how beautiful you are, you look excellent."

"She washed my hair, powdered me, the lady here lent me her powder because you always bring me the wrong sort."

I thanked the Immobile Lady with a glance and a smile.

"The nurse said your skin is too sensitive for that powder, I should bring you the ordinary sort." She laughed with her toothless mouth.

"Oh, my daughter . . . ," she waved dismissively and looked me in the eyes, as if she shouldn't have to talk with her daughter about her daughter's negligence.

"Are you in a good mood?"

"Me? A good mood? How would you feel if you were in my position?"

"Mom, what is it you don't have?"

"Death."

The Immobile Lady butted in: "You keep talking about death, please don't. I mean, what would I say, look at my legs, like two posts, I can't move, but you can, you can scurry about like a squirrel, you could be a squirrel if you only wanted, you have a good son-in-law, a good daughter, and a good granddaughter. Why do you irritate them instead of getting out of bed and going to the bathroom yourself? You don't need diapers, you don't need anything, you're a healthy woman. Look at me, look at my legs, like two posts." She seemed upset.

"You see?" my mother said.

"I'm going," I said. The invoice was waiting for me at the reception desk. We have to pay by the fifteenth, and it's better for us to pay directly and save the postage. This month she went through five hundred kuna's worth of diapers, she walked in the afternoon—a hundred kuna, baby cream—sixty kuna, the phone—zero kuna: eight and a half thousand kuna, all told. The irony is that my mother hates the Church from the bottom of her heart, but angels pay for her place in the home.

56

I MUTTERED AND rambled into the receiver.

"Have you been to the dentist's again?"

"Mmmmm."

"I can't hear you," she said.

I mumbled louder and longer: "Mmmmmmmmmmmm."

"All right, you stay in bed, look after yourself, I'll call you tomorrow, take care of yourself."

I cried.

57

Pavica and I sold five thousand euros' worth of angels in just one day.

Pino said: "If it goes on like this, I'll be able to buy myself legs."

Pavica paid the electricity bill for a whole year in advance. Ana and I went to Tuscany to celebrate Women's Day.

"Why go to Tuscany when you have Istria right in front of your nose?" Pavica asked.

"Because Istria doesn't have Florence."

We were in San Casciano in Val di Pesa. I turned on my cell phone.

"It hurts so bad, so bad, so bad, help me, my daughter!"

58

My father had only five years of schooling, he went to an Italian elementary school, and in the Yugoslav People's Army he was a warrant officer for a time. I never found out what kind of rank that was.

"When I was a warrant officer, I made all those jackasses from university line up at the edge of a stream. They were in full military gear, armed to the teeth. I ordered them to jump over the stream to see how much their fancy degrees and diplomas would help them." My father laughed. I saw tears in his red eyes as he told me with delight how all those stupid doctors, professors, and engineers almost drowned in the ice-cold water. "University won't help you. It's the school of life that counts, not books and lectures." He was given a dishonorable discharge for an offhand comment that Italian uniforms were prettier than the Yugoslav ones and that Stalin ought to be knocked off. One day later, the Tito-Stalin split occurred, and everyone had to say Stalin ought to be killed, but they never forgave him the bit about the uniforms.

My husband was standing beside me. "We're going to Istanbul," he announced cheerfully, "for five days."

She looked at us as she sucked vending-machine coffee into her toothless mouth through a pale-green straw. "Enjoy yourselves, have a good time, you deserve it," she said to my husband.

"We're actually going to Istanbul mainly because of you, they have excellent cotton."

"They do. As thick as bacon, but soft—excellent cotton."

"We'll buy some lovely underwear for you in Istanbul."

"Thank you," my mother said.

The Immobile Lady watched us numbly.

"Are you crazy?" I complained to my husband later in the car. "Why did you have to mention panties? She'll believe any hogwash you tell her. Why so over the top?"

"But we will bring her underwear from Istanbul. Their cotton is phenomenal, and their satin is cheaper than here."

"Surely we're not going to bring my mother satin panties from Istanbul?"

"No, we'll buy ourselves white satin bedclothes and spend the nights in them."

"Are you trying to say I'm an old woman who remembers a song about satin, or are you just full of lust for life?"

"You said it."

He patted me on the thigh, my husband.

59

"STOP TALKING ABOUT your deceased father and soon-to-be-deceased mother," Ana told me when we were in Florence, where they sell all those bags out in the open. We were on tenterhooks because it was so hard to choose. Florence in March isn't like Florence in July. The vendors don't yell and pull on your sleeve. "All girls of your generation have been through the same thing, it's just they haven't got time to think about it. Where would I end up if I analyzed everything my father did to me? My father and my mother. Your mom's in a lovely home . . ."

"That makes me feel guilty. She misses her bed, her nightstand, the little table with all her medicines on it, she misses home . . ."

"Oh, stop it. Every morning your mother would have you changing her pissed and crapped diapers, washing her, massaging her with ointment, and spoon-feeding her with fruit you've blended. You'd have to give her all her medicines, comb her hair, put in her false teeth . . ."

"She doesn't wear dentures anymore . . ."

". . . change her bed linen, listen to her moaning, turn her skinny, sickly body . . ."

"She's not in pain."

"A person close to ninety is always in pain. Instead of being happy that you can pay for top-quality care for the old woman in a top-notch institution, look at you!"

A board hung on the door of a restaurant with the menu written in pink chalk: *Prezzo Anticrisi, Primo Piatto, Bottiglia di acqua, caffe*, all for five euros.

"We're not in crisis, we're not going to eat here," Ana said. "But it looks great, the Italians have spirit."

The next day we drove to Greve, in Chianti. Ana is an excellent driver. We ate their phenomenal schnitzel with risotto and drank *vino tignanello* in a small osteria. We bought balsamic vinegar and authentic salami in a tiny butcher's shop. Later we came across an antique shop, and when the two English women came out we went in and each bought an old photograph showing three good-looking women from nineteen hundred and God knows when.

"We'll say they're our aunts," Ana laughed.

Ana is crazy about wine, she hardly drinks but she's a connoisseur. In Badia a Passignano we called in at the Antinori wine cellar, where we ran into a compatriot of ours, a young man from Viškovo. He helped Ana choose the wine. She chose a Solaia and a Brunello di

Montalcino, I bought a bottle of Grappa Tignanello for my husband. We returned to Florence. Both Ana and I could have spent the rest of our lives there. In the leather street we bought berets and clapped them on our heads, then we went into a small restaurant, which was completely empty. In the summertime you don't have a chance without booking a reservation. Heavy wooden tables without tablecloths, little stools. The proprietor brought us the menus.

"My mom's not happy," I said as I looked at the menu.

"You're the biggest worrier on earth. Old people are selfish, manipulative, mad that they're leaving, angry at us who are staying, envious, mean, and spiteful. Hard-hearted creatures. That's what your mother is, too."

"I threw her bed out of the apartment, I chucked her winter wardrobe in the dumpster and her summer stuff as well, I bought her a few pairs of pajamas and sweat suits, I threw her shoes in the garbage too—I left only her slippers. She kept all her documents, long-forgotten invoices, her marriage certificate, and her old health-insurance booklet in an ancient leather satchel: I disposed of everything in it except for some photographs. Later, when I looked into the satchel that had been lying around for years and saw it almost empty for the first time, I started to cry."

"Why don't you go and see a psychiatrist? It's not normal to bawl from just looking at an old satchel."

"I'm sad that the satchel and the photos are all that will be left of my mother."

"Your old mother, the satchel, and the photos might outlast you if you go on like this! Have you lost your marbles? Old mothers die. It's better her than you or, God forbid, someone you love . . ."

"I love my mom."

"Of course you love your mom, but isn't it a bit childish to be crying for a mother who's in her prime and surrounded by such phenomenal care and attention? Who'll look after you like that? Do you think Tiny will put you in such a quality home? Who knows where and how we're going to buy the farm. Enjoy life, enjoy yourself far away from your mother in diapers, woman! Grab your husband by the joystick, he'll be gone before you know it if you're teary and mopey every day. Husbands simply can't understand that."

"My husband understands me."

"But for how long? Maybe some psychiatrist will be able to tell you why you bawl, why you watch as she fades away and are afraid of death, and you think when she goes you'll be next . . ."

"Come on, that's so banal."

"Fearing death at the age of sixty is banal, but it stills gnaws at you. Why let it? The young die, the old die, what if you go on living another thirty years in sadness and despair?"

"Oh, don't scare me like that. I wish often enough I didn't exist."

"I get the impression that you simply want your old lady to die as soon as possible and get off your back, and that makes you feel guilty, so you bawl when you look at the old satchel. Admit the truth to yourself and you'll breathe more easily."

"That's not true."

Ana glanced at me. She was holding the menu. "I don't get this, what does it mean: 'Adrian Mutu eats and drinks here'? Who is this Adrian?"

"Adrian Mutu is a Romanian soccer star who plays for Florence."

Ana looked at me dumbfounded. We ordered steak. When we left, Ana discovered an ancient winestore nearby and bought a bottle of Marina Cvetić. Croatians claim the winemaker is Croatian, whereas Serbs say she's Serbian.

"I slept all night, there's some pain, but it's different, and less . . ."

I was holding the receiver with my chin and filing a fingernail.

"When are you coming?"

"Soon."

"When?"

"SOON," I yelled, "I'm so glad you're better . . ."

"Speak up a bit."

"I'm glad you're better, I'M GLAD."

"I'm glad too. Did you give Rabby some parsley? Here's the therapist for me, we'll walk around a bit, perhaps we'll go up on the next floor, and then back in the elevator."

"Bravo, Mom!"

It always touches a soft spot in me when she calls the woman who walks alongside her "the therapist."

60

BEFORE SHE BECAME a mother, my mom ran a kindergarten. She did her training in Zagreb. My grandma loved her son more than her. He was no good at school, but she paid for private lessons for him and sent him to Italy for his further education. When her husband died in a mine accident in America, she received his life insurance. She didn't buy a villa by the sea, although she could have, but a small country house in the middle of nowhere with lots of land.

"She was afraid I'd become a slut in a villa by the sea. She always beat me, with a slipper, a stick, or a cane, and tore at my hair. At the end of fifth grade she took me out of school, although the teacher emphasized that my schooling would be cost-free. 'I don't give a damn,' your grandma told my teacher, 'someone has to look after me when my head starts to damn hurt.' I was five when I went from house to house and took milk and eggs to the ladies in the villas. I was fifteen when I went off to join the partisans. If I hadn't married your father, if I hadn't given birth to you and fed you, if I hadn't needed to take care of my mother, the world would have been mine. I've never been interested in men. Remember, I've never, never, never loved your father. Never ever."

When I emptied that satchel, among the various documents I found little notes that she used to leave him on the kitchen table in the evening. She'd sleep until ten in the morning, he rose at six.

"Buy me a baguette."

How strange. They didn't talk, every day they'd exchange just two or three sentences, and still he bought her a baguette every morning for years. That was the only bread she liked, and by the time she went to the shop it would have been sold out. I was astounded that my mother asked a favor of my father, whom she hated. I was astounded that my father, who never said a single nice word about my mother in front of me, went to the market every morning and bought her a baguette.

Who were my dad and mom?

"I took a Dulcolax. Today I went poo three times. Maybe even four."

61

Attagirl, Mom. Super. You've never been interested in men. Never ever. But still, you screwed at least twice in your life. Why? To please my grandma? To please *people*? Because you thought fucking against your will would make you normal? And what about the collateral damage? Babe, you're perfectly entitled to keep repeating that you never loved men, but why do you keep saying that to me, who wouldn't exist if it hadn't been for that man, and you still expect me to bring you the right powder, the right cream, the right iced tea? What if I've never, never, never been interested in you? Never ever? But still . . . I read recently that people can be divided into the happy and the unhappy: the happy are happy whatever happens to them, and those like my mother constantly dread that something's going to devour them. There's firm evidence that people have the same kind of mirror neurons as monkeys. We imitate the people around us. We dress similarly, when we move to a different city we change the way we speak, and the same principle applies to emotions. If you mix with nervous and tense people, you'll become like that yourself. If you mingle with happy people, you'll become like them. The neurologist Richard Restak thinks I should have as little to do with my mother as possible.

"I'm not coming tomorrow," I said.

She pulled the blanket up over her head.

62

Why is my mother living when her back hurts, hemorrhoids are ravaging her butt, Faktu cream doesn't help, she has both of Father's pensions, which don't make her happy because they came too late, the carer ladies who milled around her didn't care for her, only one of them loved her, powdered her groin, combed her hair, made sure the rice was just right, cleaned the toilet, kept the glass of the shower cubicle clean, and smoked on the balcony. I can't hug her, that stresses me out of my brain, or kiss her or stroke her on the head. Does her back really hurt so much? Why is phantom pain called "phantom" if it does hurt, what is "phantom" about pain that devastates your nerves? Would my mother be depressive if she wasn't the daughter of a possessive mother, the sister of a bad brother, the wife of an evil husband, the mother of a cold daughter, the mother of a deceased daughter, and the grandmother of an absentminded granddaughter? While she was at home, my mother dreamed every night of being beaten by her mother, her brother, and my father. That must have been truly horrible, it must have been terrifying, I ought to think more, and more often, about my mother's sufferings and her feelings.

"Does something hurt?"

My husband asked me that question more and more often. I remember he was lying on his back, lighter by a grain or so (figures have never been my strong point). He looked at me in an unusual, remorseful way, I tried to be cheerful and pulled him by the toe, I don't have the faintest idea why, perhaps so he'd think I was in good spirits. I lay beside him and took his hand in mine.

"What are you thinking about?"

About the drops for her gums that I didn't buy, about not having called her today, wondering whether she's asleep, awake, groggy, angry, or sad, whether I'll buy a five-and-dime tracksuit for her, in turquoise, and have Julijana take in the legs . . .

"I'm thinking about Tuscany."

"Bravo," my husband said and turned on his side, showing his naked, white body. I covered him with the sheet. "Don't cover me up, it's hot."

The phone rang. It rang and rang. I raised the receiver although I had absolutely no idea what I'd say to her.

"I'm waiting, I've been waiting all day, why don't you call?"

"I'm in the middle of things just now."

"You're always in the middle of things when I call. I'm in pain, all day and all night, without a break."

"He is too."

"Speak louder."

"He's in pain too, my husband, it hurts so bad, so bad, so bad . . ."

"Where's it hurting?" she said with genuine concern.

"His neck," I yelled, "his neck and shoulder blade, on the left."

"Rub him with Horse Balm."

"I can't hear you, speak louder," I shouted.

"Horse Balm, Horse Balm, Horse Balm . . ." Her voice was weak.

"Rub him with Horse Balm, and say hello to him from me."

"Good," I yelled and hung up.

My husband laughed. I looked at him. "She has a mournful voice, she's not well."

"Come on, Nana's fine. Try and sleep a bit."

I watched his white back.

63

Pavica had to take her father to the doctor's that day, so I went to my shop at two in the afternoon. I don't know if you've been there. If you have, you know how small it is: the shelf with the angels, the counter that Pavica, or I, stands behind, and the small round table by the shopwindow; when people are interested but see someone else in the shop, they change their minds. If we had maybe five hundred square feet of space, more people would be able to look at the angels at the same time. Unfortunately, the rents in the city center are exorbitant. Although there's a recession, the rents of business premises haven't fallen. Along with our good range, I often think the restricted space is perhaps the key to our success. When a person goes into our store, they know that Pavica or I will give them our full attention.

There's a shop in town, the most exclusive one, which sells designer light fixtures and nothing else. I bought a weird kind of chandelier for the ceiling. Elastic tubes extend from a stainless-steel rosette like the arms of a steel octopus, nine of them, each with a different-colored glass tulip at the end, red, green, blue, purple . . . Why am I telling you this? I want to say that one often makes a good move by sheer coincidence. I bought the light fixture purely for my own enjoyment, not as a business investment. And yet it brought in a heap of money. Let me be a bit clearer. When a young mother leaves Happy Baby carrying her tot, she comes into our shop thinking she'll just pass a minute or two here because the child will get restless. But something strange always happens: every baby stares at that light fixture, I place on the table the angels that the young mother might like, she's amazed that her baby is looking at the light fixture, she asks where I bought it, and I always say it was a gift. While the baby stares, the mother pays. It's quite remarkable.

When did he come into the shop? I remember the light was on and the light fixture shone in all its beauty, it was a cold evening. It's hard to tell the time in the winter because everything's pitch-black at four in the afternoon already. We don't have a clock on the wall because the shelves take up every last bit of space, and I never look at my watch when a customer walks in. Beggars rarely come in, they know we're not going to give them anything. Not because Pavica and I are miserly—when we have a coffee in the bar we always give five kuna to the old man who just asks for one. But, like I say, the space is so limited that we haven't got room for a buyer and a beggar.

The man came in wearing a battered overcoat. His blazer was bloodied, the legs of his trousers too, and his face was covered by one or two days of gray stubble. He didn't stink.

"Sir," my voice was icy, "you can't hang around here, I'm not giving you any money, so please go out the way you came." I moved for the dark-blue telephone in the shape of an angel, which I bought in Ferrara. It always worked—the beggars thought I was going to call the police.

"I'm not a beggar, you know. I want to buy an angel."

I stopped and relaxed. I'd give him five minutes. "Please, take a look . . . ," I pointed to the Chinese angels, "these are on special, two euros apiece."

Actually they cost ten euros, but I wanted to get rid of this blood-stained beggar fast, although he didn't stink of vomit, sour wine, or cigarette smoke. I can smell people coated with nicotine a mile away.

He looked at the shelf. "Do you have children?"

I don't like talking with down-and-outs, it's too much for me to cope with. "Yes, I do. Here, maybe you'd like this yellow one?"

"No, I like the dark blue here, with the glass wings."

"Sir . . . ," I didn't know whether to smile or to stay serious, "that costs five hundred euros."

"I know, I've been here before."

"When were you here?" And I thought: *Old man, there's no way I'd forget you.*

"With Lena last year, she liked the lilac-colored angel with glass wings."

"We sold that one. Who's Lena?"

"My daughter."

"Why didn't she come? It's very hard to buy presents for girls on the off chance, and I have to advise you that we don't exchange items or give cash back. It's happened that people come several times, and each time they like some other angel more than the one they bought. That's why we don't exchange and refund anymore. So it's buy it or leave it. Why not let Miss . . ."

"Lena."

"Let Miss Lena come herself. We'll be getting new stock in next week, so the choice will be better . . ."

"Lena can't come, he killed her." The man looked at me with dry, dark-brown eyes. He unsettled me. All sorts of maniacs are out and about in Croatia these days.

I glanced toward the door. No one was about to come in. It was cold, and the square was deserted. I relaxed a bit more. If I didn't show the man I was panicking, he'd leave. I'd give him the angel if necessary. "Would you like a glass of water?" I asked politely, pointing to the table and the plastic bottle on it. The glasses were on the counter.

"Thank you," he said. "Thanks very much."

I smiled: "Thank you, no, or thank you, yes?"

"He killed her six months ago. Didn't you read in the paper?"

"Sorry, I don't read the newspapers," I said very politely now. "Could you please explain . . ."

"He killed Lena."

"Who is 'he'?"

"He is he."

I poured some water into a glass and passed it to him: "Here you are."

He drank it. "Do you have a son or a daughter?"

"A daughter."

"Then you know how much a man can love a child."

"I do, I love Tiny very much," I said, and then stopped. I didn't want to talk about her with a bloodstained stranger.

"What did Lena do? She came out of the school—the college here in the city center, do you know where it is?"

I said nothing. Of course I knew where it was.

"She came out of the school and saw three creeps kicking an old man, who a few moments before had been fishing plastic bottles out of a dumpster. I'm sure you've seen people like that."

"Of course," I said. "They're well equipped, with a rod and a sack, and some even have a lamp on their head so they can collect bottles in the dark."

"This one didn't have a lamp."

I waited.

"When my Lena saw those creeps laying into the old man, she went up and told them to stop. They stopped, sure enough, and turned on her instead. They threw my child to the asphalt in the middle of town, in broad daylight, and kicked her to death."

He looked at me with his dark, dry eyes.

"I'm sorry," I said, "I'm terribly sorry, I have a girl too, her name is Sanja, but we all call her Tiny. I can imagine how you feel . . ."

"No, you can't. Lena was everything in the world to me and my wife. I was an English teacher at school, and my wife taught Italian. Our little girl was born at the beginning of the war. Teachers' pay is poor, and so to enable her a better life we sold our little house and set up a private language school."

I watched his thin, cracked mouth as it moved. His white hands trembled.

"Our Lena was the best and most loved child in the world. As a baby she'd sleep through the night, at first we were worried and looked to see if she was still breathing—that's how calmly she slept.

My wife breastfed her for a year, was careful what she ate, and little Lena developed well, and when she was one year old my late mother took care of her most days." He wiped his wet forehead.

I was also hot. I almost choked. I poured myself a glass of water too.

"My mother was also crazy about Lena. She sewed little dresses for her, took her out in the stroller, and when we came to pick her up she'd often say: 'I'm not giving up my little Lena.' Our school didn't last long, the taxes crushed us and we went bust, but we found a way. We tutored school students in their homes, and we inherited my mother's apartment. I'd be lying if I said we had a hard life. Lena was a wonderful child."

"I understand," I said.

"She was the best in her school, she had a talent for languages but was also good at math. She planned to go to London together with Renata, who she'd been friends with since the beginning of elementary."

"Ah," I went, "now I see."

"And then she ran into those fiends."

"That's the word, 'fiends.' Underage criminals are roaming our streets more and more. Fiends indeed."

"No one came to her aid. People stayed clear of those monsters as they killed my little Lena. She lay dead on the asphalt for perhaps half an hour before anyone called an ambulance. The autopsy showed that his steel-toed Doc Martens had broken dear Lena's skull . . ."

"Calm down, do please calm down." I took him to the chair. "Sit down, have a little water."

"Two of them were sentenced, but he was released. The forensic expert couldn't determine whose steel-toed Doc Martens actually killed her. The judge said they were all young, and he was from a good family, a first offender, he ought to be given another chance, and the little fellow was hardly more than a child. His father is a judge. So he got away with it."

"Our courts are terrible," I agreed, "an absolute shambles. There are killers out and about."

"Minus one. I found out what I needed to know. I followed him day and night, I knew more about him than he himself. My wife is a wonderful, calm person—she supported me. 'We have nothing to lose,' she said, 'and we can still do something for Lena.'"

The square was completely empty. Gentle rain was falling. Where did the rain come from? Did they say on TV that it would rain? I don't watch TV, but Pavica always watches the weather forecast.

"I organized a sack, a lamp, a cap, and a rod. And waited. I waited for four months. He was always in a group. Until today. When I saw him coming out of the school alone, I called him over. He came up to me: 'What can I do for you, mister?' He was very friendly. A blond, delicate boy. He was wearing ordinary shoes. 'Please, my boy, could you help me get that bottle out of the dumpster?' He smiled, took off his jacket, turned around, and put his head in the dumpster. Then I drove the rod into his neck. He and I were alone, you see, there's no one outdoors. He gurgled. I pulled the rod out of his neck and rammed it in again, and stabbed him with it a third time. Then I pulled it out and threw it into the dumpster, and him with it. He was a slight boy, I don't know if he weighed even one hundred and thirty pounds." He placed the empty glass on the counter and left the shop.

When I got home—we don't have a computer in the shop—I googled "assigned counsel" and "murder out of revenge." The man could get forty years.

"You're not looking well."

"Mom, I'm tired."

The home was decorated with brightly colored paper streamers.

"Dressed-up children came yesterday afternoon. Each of us had to give them a red chocolate heart. I hope they had fun. I didn't give them the heart."

"Mom! Why not?"

"Because I ate it."

64

"I DREAMED THAT Rabby died. It made me cry and cry. Why doesn't anyone come?"

65

"Rabby said to me: 'Nana, I died because she didn't give me any parsley.' I ate yellows today, but I still haven't done a number two. Bring me Horse Balm. And Tiger Balm too, it cools."

66

"I ate a whole bowl of greens, Katica was here, she brought me a big bottle of tea, I went poo twice, I went to the bathroom by myself, I saved three diapers. Satisfied?"

"I won't be coming today . . ."

"Why not? Is Tiny coming? Who's coming?"

"Nobody today. Did you go for a walk?"

"I'm not telling you if I went for a walk."

"Mom, don't be childish."

"Why isn't anyone coming?"

"Because we came yesterday."

"Tiny came yesterday, you didn't."

"Okay, I didn't. Now did you go for a walk?"

"Yes. I was up on the next floor, and then we came down in the elevator."

"You went for a walk? How did you go for a walk when today is Sunday? Your therapist doesn't come on Sundays."

"I thought today was Monday."

67

I need a husband, I thought when I was twenty-six. Men are all the same, men are a sex aid, they help you come better and more easily. I need a father for my children. He should be tall and handsome, with beautiful eyes, strong biceps, and broad shoulders. Only that way will my son be handsome, with beautiful eyes, strong biceps, and broad shoulders. I'll have two handsome, tall sons, two Indian braves with straight, black hair, and I'll stand between them and show all my teeth to the camera. When I have children, *people* will know I'm normal, a woman like every other, a young mom, one of millions.

I told that to my husband, back when he wasn't my husband.

"I'll be the father of your children," he said and looked at me with that look of his. I'm sorry I can't show you those warm, brown eyes.

"You can't be the father of my children because you're not tall, you haven't got broad shoulders or black, straight hair, your muscles are soft . . ."

"I'll train, I'll grow, I'll straighten my hair and dye it black."

"You and I are like brother and sister, whenever I screwed anyone I came running to you straightaway and told you everything, we laughed together about all my lovers, you know everything about each of them, and you know what I did with them. You're more than a brother for me, you're my one best friend, as good as any girl friend."

"Where does it say that best friends can't be fathers?"

We screwed for months because I wanted to see if he could have children at all, I didn't want a man whose sperm was sluggish, whom I'd have to console because of that so he wouldn't go and hump somebody else to keep from feeling bad. When I got pregnant, I told my one, and best, friend and future husband that I wanted to get married. The child had to have a father and a mother and had to be born in wedlock.

"Your word will always be my command," he said, so we were married in a medieval town on a hill. I found it a bit awkward that my brother, best friend, and husband were fucking me every night and day, but I got used to it over time. My daughter is tall, and her long, straight hair is almost black.

"Tell me, who does my daughter take after? Who's her father? You know you can tell me everything."

She bears so little resemblance to her father, it's almost uncanny. But my husband is still my daughter's father, bear that in mind when you meet him on the street. And a perfect father: he buys her the perfume that's currently most expensive, he knows all her secrets, all his CDs are also hers, he buys her panties and bras—my husband is my daughter's best friend. And I'd thought only the beautiful women that mom likes are happy in love.

"Let me have that blue angel."

"The lady's daughter was here yesterday."

I glanced at the Immobile Lady. She was staring at the blaring TV.

"That's nice," I said to my mother's bleary eyes.

"Cover me up."

I covered her up.

"Cover up my feet."

I covered up her feet.

"Cover me up."

I covered her up again.

"Cover up my feet."

I covered up her feet.

"Cover me up."

The Pink Coat came into the room smiling and holding greens.

68

He gets up earlier. Every morning before we go to work, he makes me coffee and puts it on the night table. He opens the curtains so I can look at the dark-red flowers while I'm sipping it. What did I do to deserve this? I'll tell you, although I shouldn't, so let this just be between you and me: I'm not much good in bed. I don't know if I've really laughed more than fifty times in my life, and I'm not allowed to eat salty food, so we rarely eat in restaurants. I mostly make turkey medallions, it says on the packet that they fry in five minutes; we often eat pancakes too, I'm nuts about them, and that's all. I guess. I have a housekeeper, so I don't clean and don't iron. Sometimes I worry that one fine morning, or perhaps late afternoon, my husband will come to his senses.

"What did he see in you?" my mother asked me.

"What did you see in me?" I asked him.

"Cut the crap."

"Do you think we can go on vacation? She won't die while we're gone, will she?"

The head nurse laughed into the receiver. "My dear, we look death in the face every day here. Your mother is far, far from it, she's simply drifting into senility. You've known her for so long you don't see it. Relax, go on vacation, we're here."

"You've switched off her buzzer."

"She kept ringing every five minutes, if she was really unwell we would have gone to her . . ."

"How do you know how she is if you can't see her?"

"What do you mean 'can't see her'?"

"Well, you can't see her if you're far away, she could get nauseous, be sick, and drown in her own vomit before you come . . ."

"Perhaps you're not aware that all the rooms are equipped with CCTV, and there are also microphones. Nothing happens in this building that isn't monitored twenty-four hours a day. Everything's under control, including your mom."

"Sorry. Thank you so much."

"You're most welcome."

I called her: "I talked with the head nurse, she said you're in excellent form."

"Tomorrow is bathing, and bathing hurts."

"Mom, how the hell can you be afraid of water?"

She hung up.

69

"If I die while you're away, put Rabby into good hands."

70

"When did you start drinking, Mom?"

"It's an illness like any other. My dad was ill with it too. If it hadn't been for your possessive grandma, who I had to look after, if it hadn't been for my brother, who was given an education although he was dumber than me, if your grandma had allowed me an education, if I hadn't married because your grandma forced me to, if your father hadn't made me quit at the kindergarten after the second child, if I hadn't given birth to you and breastfed you, I could have become someone. I pulled through without medicine. The doctor said to me: 'You're an intelligent woman, you don't need that. Never in my life have I met such a lucid woman. You just need to tell yourself: "I'll drink tomorrow."' And I said to myself: 'I'll drink tomorrow,' and I still say it to myself today, and I haven't drunk for forty years. I'll drink tomorrow."

"You stopped when I was twenty."

"You're a nasty, vengeful person. Alcoholism is an illness, not a vice."

"I'm not coming today."

"Why not?"

"Rabby is sick, I'm taking her to the vet's."

"What's wrong with her?"

"It's terminal, we'll have to put her down."

She cried. In a strange, creaky way.

71

My grandma held my hand in hers. A storm was blowing—I don't know if it was a sirocco or a northerner—Father was out somewhere, and we went from door to door. Grandma's gray wisp of hair peeked out from under her kerchief, she weighed about seventy pounds, was wearing a black dress, as always, almost to the ground, and had slippers on her feet. She held a candle and matches in her hand. My mother had gone out of the house drunk and told us she was going to hang herself. When a storm is howling, the only place you can hang yourself in that small, seaside town is in a cellar, so we opened the cellar doors, all of them were unlocked, and went from one to the next, there were about twenty of them, and we went into each and every one, lit the candle, and looked at the hooks on the ceilings. Was she hanging? Was she not? Was she hanging? Was she not? She wasn't hanging. There was a body covered with a dirty blanket in the corner of one cellar . . . There came the sound of snoring . . . We uncovered the body. It wasn't my mom, but old Andre. We covered him up again. The stream had turned into a torrent. We crossed the small bridge and walked close to the hotel, hiding from the rain because we didn't have an umbrella. There in the canal, near the shop, lay my mother. Thin arms, thin legs, a dark-red face. Grandma was angry and relieved at the same time, and we carried my mom home. My father was somewhere, my sister upstairs. We dragged her into the bedroom, washed her face, arms, and legs, and put a metal basin next to the bed, tonight she'd bring up bile, liver, and blood. In the morning she'd be angry, sullen, or broken. She'd lie all day with the blanket over her head, or sit quietly in the kitchen by the stove, or snarl at us because there was no money. Grandma and I had discovered bottles of rum in the house—we tipped them out and I threw the empties into the garbage. The small ones with rum for making cakes and the half-liter ones. They were in the dirty linen, the clean linen, the cistern, and the cellar. Never, never, could we have found all the bottles. How did she manage to buy all that rum? My mom didn't work, but there were always good people who loaned her money although they knew she'd never return it.

"Has Rabby died?"

"Not yet. We're taking good care of her. We give her medicine every half an hour, day and night."

"My poor Rabby."

72

You'll never see me celebrating my birthday in a restaurant that looks like a real seaside tavern. The people of the north Croatian coast, the Primorci, are reclusive folk. Nothing is known about them. Slavonians love their pork sausages and tamburitzas. And the people of Dalmatia love chard and sad songs about dads, gramps, old mas, and maidens who wait for years, longing for their captain to return. But who are the Primorci? Nobody has ever investigated why the women drink, throw themselves into wells, or overdose on tablets, and why the men don't talk about their drunken wives or those who have jumped into wells. The Primorci are uncommunicative, which is such a shame, I think. If they spoke more I might know today who my father was and who my mother was.

"Tiny told me Rabby is better. Who's going to come today?" her voice sounded somehow broken. Yes, broken.

"Nobody!"

73

ALCOHOLISM IS AN illness and needs to be treated. But how? My grandmother thought her daughter's alcoholism could be cured by yelling, howling, pulling her hair, crying, swearing, screaming, slapping, cursing, and imploring. My father thought his wife's alcoholism could be cured by his own alcoholism, by laying into my skinny, half-dead mother, by growling, swearing, sneering, smashing things, yelling, beating the children, licking my neck, squeezing other men's wives, dancing with girls who could have been his children, and locking up his daughters in a small room. I thought my mother's alcoholism could be cured by talking, crying, and throwing plates at her drunken head.

The phone rang. I goggled at the number. Should I pick up the receiver, or wait for it to stop ringing?

"Who's going to come today?" her voice sounded imploring.

"Nobody!"

74

THE IMMOBILE LADY watched me. It was very hot. Her diapers were white. Again, I wasn't able to hug my mother, or kiss her.

"Cover me up," said the spindly infant in the turquoise plastic.

I covered her up.

"The blanket hurts."

She looked at me imploringly, with the eye of a cooked fish. She looked at me, looked at me, and looked at me, expecting a kiss, a hug, or a pat.

"For the life of me, I can't kiss her, I can't hug her, I can't stroke her on the head—I can't, I simply can't!" I told my husband in the car.

"Calm down, she doesn't expect that of you. Primorci are reserved people who don't show their feelings. Wife, do you love me at all?" He looked at me and laughed with his eyes.

"No," I said, "who could love a Dalmatian blabbermouth?"

75

"Why doesn't somebody help me? Why doesn't somebody kill me?"

She tossed and turned in her bed and constantly demanded that we cover her feet or her back, turn her on her side, raise the head end of the bed, adjust the pillow . . .

"Calm down, Mom."

"Why don't you kill me, what's the point of all this?"

The lady in the corner said: "Don't believe her, she's not in pain, she slept all night, breathed evenly, and didn't budge. Look at my legs, like two posts, the nurses turn me all night, every two hours, I don't sleep at all, but she's always sleeping, day and night, she only complains when you come, as soon as she sees you she starts to scream."

As the Immobile Lady spoke, I looked into my mother's pale eyes.

"What did she tell you? I'm sure she said I'm not in pain, that I sleep all night long . . ."

"The lady said the food here is good and that she went to the restaurant today. Maybe you could make your way to the restaurant tomorrow . . ."

My mother switched her gaze to my husband. "Why don't you tell her that I'm in pain and that I can't walk? You're the only one who believes me."

"Nana, I believe you, but you know best how hard it is with your daughter. Let her speak, and you can still do as you wish."

"Would you be so kind as to tell the nurse to give me something for this pain, some drops . . . or could you take me home."

"Home?" I said. "How do you mean 'home'?"

"At home in my bed everything would be easier, when people are at home they can help themselves." She looked at my husband.

I slowly breathed in and out again.

"What's up with you." The fish-eye turned toward my eyes.

"Arrhythmia."

"Why don't you go to the doctor's? You should take care of yourself."

"She's perfectly okay," my husband said. "She's too nasty for anything to be wrong with her, isn't that right, Nana?"

She smiled: "That's right."

We left the room.

"Let's go round to the other side and look through the window to see if she's sitting and drinking coffee, or lying down."

We peered in through the window. She was lying there and looked us straight in the eyes.

76

If I could, I'd buy my grandmother's house from my uncle and move there. It's surrounded by meadows, sheep probably still graze there today, little bells tinkle around their woolly necks, the air is full of thyme, with the sea nearby yet at a comfortable distance, and a stone-paved yard with a well. My father was obsessed with the thought that his mother loved his brother more than him. Grandmother lived alone for about twenty years, and never once did my father visit her. He spoke with hatred about the woman who would leave everything to *him*. Him—that was his despised brother. My uncle loved his mother, always took her gifts, wrote her postcards and letters when he was at sea, and took her bread and meat when he was on shore leave.

"That's all self-serving, pure self-interest—he'd kill his own father and mother for two dinars. He fusses over her because she's going to leave everything to him."

What could my grandmother leave my uncle? That country house and several acres of land.

"He knows why he fusses over her, he knows very well why he fusses over that damn cow."

I'm sure he wanted to say "bitch"—"cow" is no big insult. A cow is more dull than vicious, more stupid than malicious; a calculating attitude and hatred are foreign to a cow; a cow certainly wouldn't have left everything she had to just one son; bitches do that, all women are bitches, all of them love one son more than the other. Bitch, bitch, bitch.

"Cow, cow, cow," he said.

"You know, I'm a patient woman, I can put up with a lot, but I can't take this anymore."

"Mom, just grin and bear it."

"Bear what?"

"The pain."

She cried.

"I can't. I can't go on. Tell them to give me something."

"I'll tell them."

"When?"

"Now, I'm going to the pain clinic right now."

"Go there, I beg you, just go."

The nurse heard me out. "I understand, but you have to understand me too. I'm by myself, and without the doctor's permission I can't do anything."

"Call the doctor, call anyone, give me his phone number."

She called the doctor. She brought her a Tramacet.

77

"My franjo is calling me," Grandmother said one morning.

She didn't live to see the next day.

My mother minded Tiny so I could go to the funeral. My father didn't go. I didn't go to his either, but that wasn't until much, much later. When I came back to their place from the funeral, no one asked me anything. My mother showed with a motion of her hand that *he* was there, lying in his room. Tiny was asleep in the main bedroom. She told me in the children's room that *he* had been lying in bed all day the way he lay when he was recovering from a drinking spree, but she didn't think he was drunk. She whispered this and smoked half a cigarette. She never smoked in front of him and never smoked a whole cigarette; she'd flick off the ember, drop it into the big pocket of her apron, and two hours later she'd light up again. She thought she heard him crying—whining, to be exact. Sobbing.

"You won't believe it, but he kept calling out to her and repeating: 'Mom, Mom, Mom, Mom . . .'"

"I don't believe it," I said. "That's certainly news. He's crying, he's able to cry, his *mom* has died."

That cheered me up.

"How are things?" I shouted into the receiver. "The tablet helps, it's a big one, huge, it has to help, it's a combination of Ultram and Tylenol, if it doesn't kill your pain I don't know what will."

"I'm better, thank you."

"You're better—just 'better,' or well?"

"I'm not 'well,' but I'm better."

"I can't go on like this," I said to Tiny. "The old crock will have us all on the therapist's couch, or worse."

"Mom, why put on such a performance? She's far, far away from us, almost half an hour's drive, hear her out, and then hang up. Surely you can stand those two minutes."

"Two minutes!" I yelled. "How can you not understand that my damned conversation with her has been going on for almost sixty years. I've been listening to her all my life, I can't do it anymore."

"I've been listening to you all my life, and it hasn't hurt me. Relax, Mom, I'll go up there today."

78

THE COW DIDN'T leave everything to just the one son. She died without writing a will.

I called her. It took a long time, and then there were strange sounds in the receiver. A thumping and banging, and a heavy sigh, followed by the sound of hanging up.

I felt my heart flutter in my throat.

79

WHY IS MY dead father on my mind so often? I shouldn't give any more thought to him, I should blow my nose long and hard, clear it, wipe it, and clean it well to free it of all smells. Shakespeare said that to mourn a misfortune that is past and gone is the quickest way to draw new misfortune on. Or at least I think it was Shakespeare.

My sister asked me as we were sitting in front of the Oncology Department, on the small terrace almost on the road, surrounded by patients at death's door, fighting for breath or light: "You haven't seen Father for years, but you remember how he smells?"

"No," I said, "I've forgotten everything."

"Kill me, kill me, kill me, I can't go on like this anymore."

I looked into her savage, distorted face.

"I'll go and tell the nurse . . ."

"When?"

"A bit later."

"A bit later . . . ," she groaned, "why don't you go straightaway?"

I went to the pain clinic.

"There's no doctor, I'm not allowed to give her anything she hasn't been prescribed, you'll have to be patient, the phantom pain will go away when the Prozac starts to take effect, your mother is very depressive, but the psychiatrist said she's all there, she's not senile, just depressive. Please be patient. Don't go back to her now, you'll only unsettle her, the lady in the same room as your mother says she only gets restless when she sees you, otherwise she lies there calmly and sleeps . . ."

I went out of the building through the lower exit. From the road I could see my mother in bed. She was lying on her side with her back to me, watching the door of the room.

Waiting for me.

80

When my mother left my father, I sold her house and we sold our apartment. Then I bought the little house where we live and a studio apartment in a condo for my mother—in my name, so that it not be considered marital property.

She said: "For the first time in my life I have my own key."

I ordered a second lock because she lived in mortal fear of him finding her, even in a large city on the tenth floor of a high-rise, behind a door with no name plaque.

"He'll find me, he'll find me, he can't get over it, I dream of him every night, and he beats me. He beats me, and my mother beats me, and my brother beats me . . ."

"Just don't start drinking again," I said.

"I'll drink tomorrow."

About ten years later, my husband and I got into a financial tangle, so we sold the condo where my mother was living and rented a small apartment for her.

She didn't object: "If it suits you, my children, it's fine with me, the main thing is that we're together."

Several years later my mother sold the grave where her mother lay so we could repay the loan.

"It worries me a bit what to do with her bones, that's the only thing that worries me. Can you ask what we should do with the bones?"

I didn't ask. What do I feel for my mother? Have I forgiven her? Can anything ever be forgiven? What is forgiveness?

Wasn't it Ambrose Bierce who said, "Forgiveness is a word we thought up so that the sinner thinks we've forgotten"?

I remember every day. Should I forgive and forget because my mother was now being good to me? My mother was being good to me because it was her way of helping herself. A selfish old lady, she always just looked to her own interest.

"Ma'am, you worry too much," the head nurse told me.

We were standing at her bedside, she was breathing with difficulty.

"You see, she's not in pain."

"But she's straining to breathe, could it be pneumonia? Why doesn't she wake up?"

The head nurse gave me a big smile. "She doesn't have pneumonia, and she's not waking up because you asked that we give her a painkiller. You're never satisfied: it doesn't suit you when your mom sleeps, it doesn't suit you when she screams." She patted me on the shoulder with her well-groomed hand.

"I'd like to have a mother who's alert and not in pain."

"Be patient, your mother's depressive, the psychiatrist says the Prozac needs some time to act. You'll see, in the springtime you'll be walking together in the park. Have you noticed that we're building a bar, a fitness studio, and a hairdresser's in front of the home? There will also be a dance hall . . ."

"Thank you," I said, "thank you so much, you're very kind."

81

I COULD ONLY kiss my mother on her birthday and for the New Year. And I had to force myself. We'd look at each other darkly, and then get it over and done with. I'd give her a dry kiss on her dry face, and she'd kiss the air beside my cheek. It's not that I'm unfeeling. I keep two photographs on the fridge door of the ladies who should have been my moms. Ana calls me "my darling" and makes me salt-free salsa, and Marica lives in Belgrade and is over ninety but always chirps into the receiver when she hears my voice. Why aren't they my moms? I kiss them as soon as I see them, I'm calm and cheerful when I'm with them, they think I'm young and still have lovely, fulfilling years ahead of me. I also love Dr. Mirjana Krizmanić and her books. I'll also put her photo on the fridge.

I feel guilty because I don't wash my mother's butt with my own hands, I don't change her diapers, I don't comb what's left of her hair, I don't massage her white back, I don't cut her fingernails and toenails, whenever a nursing attendant at the home does her diaper, I leave the room. I have absolutely no idea what my mom smells like. The nursing attendant prattles to my mother while she moans in pain, she's always moaning, I hear it through the closed door of the room while I stand trembling out in the corridor.

I called her.

"Where have you been all this time, when are you coming, is anyone coming today, what day is it, what's the time? It hurts so bad, so bad, so bad, if only you knew how much it hurts. It hurts so much, I'm dying here in terrible pain . . ."

Her voice was weak, but she still snarled.

"I'll come."

"When?!"

"This afternoon."

She slammed down the receiver or it fell out of her hand, and I would have poured myself a stiff drink had I not been on Praxiten.

82

I TRIED CALLING her. It rang for a long time, but she didn't answer. I tried again half an hour later, in vain.

I punched in the head nurse's number. "How's my mom? She's not answering."

The head nurse was always in a phenomenally good mood: "She's not answering because she's sleeping. We gave her something."

"How is she?"

"She's well. How else could she be? Your mother is really well, perhaps a bit pampered. You fuss over her too much, you should visit less often and do something you enjoy for a change, don't let her manipulate you and spoil your mood, she's well."

"She told me she was in terrible pain."

The head nurse laughed: "Relax, we monitor her condition, she's slowly going senile, she keeps repeating like a robot, 'It hurts so bad, so bad, so bad,' but she isn't in pain."

I began to visit less often.

83

"I DREAMED THAT you were dead and Rabby hopped around on your belly as you lay there. How is Rabby?"

84

HER ARMS WERE as thin as sticks. Her legs too. She was wearing little pink socks. I had bought them for her. When? Where?

"Why can't I die, can you answer me that?"

She wasn't tense, she just looked at me with those cooked-fish eyes.

"Mom, you can't die because you're not ill."

I couldn't tell if her toothless mouth was contorted into a sneer—or crying without tears.

"My daughter . . ."

A nursing attendant came into the room with a bowl full of an orange-colored mixture. She raised the head end of the bed. My mother howled.

"Come on, Granny, don't complain. Now it's time for din-din, and then we'll have a nice nap."

My mother looked at me as she opened her mouth, swallowed the orange mixture, and opened her mouth again.

"I'll be off then," I waved cheerfully while her mouth was full of the mixture, "see you tomorrow."

85

"Two ladies took me to the restaurant today because you said I have to eat at the restaurant."

She scratched herself on the back and adjusted the lilac blanket.

"Mom, you have to move around, you mustn't stay lying or you'll get bedsores. Believe me, there are worse things than what you're going through at the moment . . ."

"Damn you!"

I recoiled. She didn't look at me, she just pulled at the blanket and tried to turn onto her side.

"What did you say?"

"I said: Damn you."

I was surprised to feel tears in my eyes. "Why are you saying this to me?" It was unbelievable, I almost burst aloud into tears.

"Because you don't believe me, those two only dragged me to the restaurant because you don't believe me. I fell when they made me sit at the table there, and I screamed so loud that everyone ran away, and a lady who was pushing her rollator even fell herself when she heard me scream . . ."

"Mom!"

"And then those two returned me to bed, and I yelled and screamed, and they brought me a big, chunky tablet. They said it was a combination of Ultram and Tylenol, and that it would calm me down—but it didn't—so I also got three green ones."

"You amaze me. Your behavior!"

"*Your* behavior! I want to go home . . ."

"Home?"

"Home. I want to die at home in my own bed, I want to see Rabby one last time."

My mother didn't know that we'd given the key of her apartment back to the landlady and that Rabby now lived with us. When she came out of her cage, she went and peed behind the toilet.

"Mom, you need care day and night, you simply can't be at home until you're better. If only you ate a bit more . . ."

"Don't go on about food, you're always pushing me to eat . . ."

"Mom, you have to recover, regain your strength . . ."

"I want to die, everyone dies except me."

"Who's died?"

"They've all died, the politician Savka Dapčević-Kučar has died too."

"Who told you that?"

"Meri. She was here this morning." Meri used to be one of her carer ladies, I don't remember the how-many-eth. "Meri kissed me."

"That's nice, Mom, people like you."

"People have always liked me. She brought me peach iced tea, body lotion, and tissues. Did you bring tissues?"

"I did, in a box, so you can take them out more easily."

"I can't take the tissues out of the box, see, my hands are hopeless, feel my fingers . . ."

I touched her ice-cold fingers. "Your fingers are fine, if only you exercised . . ."

"I'm not going to hold back anymore, I've been a decent woman, and now all this is happening to me. I want you to know that the next time it hurts I'm going to scream so loud that you'll hear me even at home, I'll shriek until they zonk me out . . ."

"Mom, why are you doing this to me? We all want to help . . . If only you exercised and walked more, if you went to the toilet at least once a day you wouldn't need diapers, you'd feel less helpless, if you went to the restaurant by yourself, it's ten steps from your room . . ."

She shut her eyes and gently sobbed.

I stroked her hand.

"It was terrible how your mom screamed, terrible. If I was at least healthy like her . . . my legs are like two posts, and the nurses turn me day and night, every two hours . . . I went for a back operation, I think I was strong and straight beforehand, and now look at me . . . but I don't scream. She's so pampered, everyone fusses over her . . . I've asked them to move me to a different room."

The TV blared, a middle-aged man was telling his wife that he was leaving because he didn't love her anymore. She cried.

I went out and looked for the head nurse.

"My mom said she felt sick at the restaurant today."

"Sick?"

"Or suddenly unwell—she fell and screamed with pain."

"She didn't fall, she just slipped out of the arms of the nursing attendants. We tried to take her to the restaurant so she'd perk up a bit. She's been so very restless recently."

"Why?"

"Why? You can never tell with old people."

"She said she was in excruciating pain."

"They all want a bit of attention, a few tender words. Kiss her and stroke her on the head, and it will all pass, they're like children."

"Do you think I should go back to the room and comb her hair a bit?"

The nurse laughed. "You do so much for her, someone's always visiting, she has all of you are around her. No, we can comb her, just you go home and relax. She has everything she needs."

I went out via the upper exit, returned to the building, and left through the lower exit. My mother was lying on her side looking toward the door of the room. Yes, I ought to have gone back and combed her hair. A nursing attendant in a pink coat went into the room carrying a bowl full of green mash. She placed it on the night table and left again. My mother was asleep.

86

I LEFT THE stench of garlic and white wine long ago. I went away. Some go, some stay. Do they really go? Where do they go? Every evening when I see the pile of dishes in the kitchen sink I think my late father will come in through the glass door of the terrace and beat me and my husband for living in such a chaotic mess, amid mountains of unwashed dishes and masses of books. Naturally, my dead father will never come to my house, he didn't come even while he was alive. I left my father, in a way, while my sister stayed. My story is a happy one.

And yet, can anyone flee from their father?

Can anyone flee from a dead father?
When is a dead father dead?

87

ANA CAME INTO the shop. She brought a heap of Chinese angels that glowed in the dark. Five euros a piece.

"Has someone kicked the bucket? Your mom?" Ana laughed.

"She still refuses to go to the hairdresser's, and she hasn't put in her dentures or worn her glasses since she's been at the home."

"She's sending you the message that she's given up on life, and that it's your fault. She wants you to get her out and take her home, for you to be one-on-one again. Don't fall for it, babe." Ana looked at me.

I laughed.

"Come on, fight for your right to a life. If she doesn't want teeth, she doesn't want teeth. If she doesn't want glasses, she doesn't want glasses. If she doesn't want the hairdresser, she doesn't want the hairdresser. Why the fuck should it bother you? It's either her or you."

"Last night she screamed, she screamed so much that the nurses said they'd transfer her."

"Where to?"

"The inpatient clinic. Her back is hurting in a totally different way, her fingers go numb, sometimes her pain is so piercing that she feels she's about to die. She demands that we take her home, and one of her eyes is constantly shut."

"Do calm down," Ana piled the angels on the shelf. "Shall I go and get us a macchiato?"

"I asked a nurse what the inpatient clinic is. She told me it's a part of the home where the old people are under better observation. Everything's the same except there are four women in the room and there's almost no privacy."

"What do you mean 'no privacy'?" Ana placed a huge dark-red angel in the shopwindow. "Babe, this one is so good I'd even take it home. Pino is king. Look, a dark-red angel with a tuft of green hair, a blue mouth, black teeth—what will customers see in black teeth and the gold varnish on its little nails?—what do you mean 'no privacy'?"

"The door of the room is wide open twenty-four hours a day so they can keep a better eye on the patients."

"Or leave them in the draft so they die quicker."

"Oh, lay off!" I said. "My mom's not well. They take good care of the patients, each of them brings in almost nine thousand kuna per month."

"You're right. How about I hop over and get us macchiato?"

"Some ladies are in the inpatient clinic for years."

"And sleep for years in a room whose door is wide open?"

"They haven't decided yet when they're going to move her. If she's calm she can stay where she is, but if she's restless she'll go to the inpatient clinic."

"I don't understand. Why don't they sedate her? We keep hearing on TV that pain is an illness too, that pain has to be combated, that today we all have the right to await death without pain . . . But your old lady's howling away with pain, and you even pay for it. If I were you, I'd go up there and give them hell. How about I hop over and get us some macchiatos?"

"She's not in pain, it's just a phantom sensation, they told me she's going senile, and they're always smiling from ear to ear . . ."

"All shopkeepers smile like that. There are studies that show it's one of the hardest jobs, with that perpetual smiling. Stewardesses, saleswomen, nurses, nursing attendants, chiropodists, waiters—all those poor people are constantly grinning, and then they snap."

"She's losing touch with reality . . ."

"Lucky her. Now I'm going to get those macchiatos."

88

"SHE'S BEEN SCREAMING a lot recently, it's so hard to sleep alongside your mother, she keeps howling, 'It hurts so bad, so bad, so bad' . . . I can't stand it anymore, I'm not so well myself. My legs are like two posts, the nurses turn me day and night, every two hours, but I don't yell . . . someone is always coming to see her, all the time, and she's never satisfied. My daughter can't come because she has two small children, and my son can't either because he works in Italy, you know, I sold my apartment so I could pay for this here, but I have no peace, the money just melts away, and I wonder what will become of me when it's all spent . . ."

"Your children will help you."

"What's she saying? Is she telling you again that I'm bad?"

"Mom, the lady says her daughter can't come because she has small children, and her son works in Italy . . ."

"I can't hear, what did she say?"

"She said her daughter can't come because she has small children, and her son works in Italy," I yelled.

"You don't need to holler at me . . ."

"How are you?" I shouted all the same.

She contorted her toothless mouth. "When are you going to Istanbul?"

"Tomorrow."

"Have a good time and tell Tiny to collect my pension. If I die the money will be lost . . ."

"You're not going to die."

She closed her eyes.

Some people travel, videotape their trips, write travel pieces, list all the churches and mosques they've been to, the exhibitions they've seen, and the souvenirs they've bought. My husband and I are constantly traveling, but I can't remember all the major cities I've been to because I don't travel in order to visit famous buildings but to escape from the people closest to me. When I'm out of the country and strolling along unfamiliar streets, I watch the people and sniff the air. I love Vienna in December, with the horses in the rain waiting for customers. There's a bar in Mariahilf where they serve quality loose-leaf tea, next to it is a jewelry store, and there's a gallery in Burggasse where I bought a handbag made of the drum of a washing machine. In 5 Oceanos, in Lisbon, I watched a beautiful young black woman clobbering a lobster on the head with a wooden club. 5 Oceanos is by the waterside, near the enormous bridge; I also love Sicily in April, orange groves, dormant Etna, or the fair in Muggia, where the clothes are usually sold by young Chinese women who speak Croatian, Italian, and Slovenian perfectly. I'm primitive, I'm not interested in centennial churches or exhibitions, although I've seen all the Picassos in the world. When you're traveling, the most beautiful feeling is that you're far from home, that the plane could crash and it wouldn't matter, that your mom knows she mustn't call you, that she could be sick but even with the best will in the world you can't rush off to the home, that the phone in the hotel room never rings because no one knows which hotel you're in, and that the streets beyond the cities' pedestrian zones still look like places inhabited by real people, not dolls obsessed with Armanis and Gabbanas. My husband and I always tell people we're getting back the day after we actually do. It's a wonderful feeling to be home without anyone knowing, neither Tiny, nor friends, nor my mother, because your home becomes like a hotel in a foreign country, you can spend the day in pajamas, and if the phone rings we don't pick up the receiver. If it were mine to decide, I'd die on some trip.

On the way back from Istanbul, in the plane, we realized that we'd forgotten to buy the underwear for my mom, although they were on sale on every street corner. I'd spent two hours in a shop for underwear, pajamas, and lingerie without even thinking of my mother. The saleswoman persistently tried to persuade me to buy special underpants that lift the buttocks, I refused, and now I'm sorry. We'll go to Istanbul again, I'll pig out again on rice pudding, and I'll buy those panties.

"I feel absolutely terrible," I said to my husband in the plane.

"You're crazy," he laughed. "We'll buy Grandma Turkish underwear at the market, do you really think she'll see the difference?"

"How could I forget her like that?"

There was no Turkish underwear at the market, so my husband bought Camel brand underpants. She didn't notice the difference and said thank you. I had my two lovely pairs of Turkish pajamas shortened and taken in, and I folded them and laid them in her dresser.

The next day, I arrived to see my mother's body in the white-striped turquoise pajamas. She looked like a broken puppet.

"Mom, are your pajamas too warm?"

"It hurts so bad, so bad, so bad, so bad . . ."

89

When do people grow up? When should they grow up? Is it not unbelievable that I, at the age of sixty, still dread my living mother and constantly see my dead father yelling, belting me, swearing, threatening, growling, throttling, spitting, lashing out . . . At the age of sixty, I'm still a little girl afraid of her mean father. Am I exaggerating? I mean, the old man is in the ground at last, lying between rosemary and lavender, sheep bleat next to his grave, and everything's just the way he wanted it, he chose the location and the type of marble himself; his arms are now flimsy bones, never again will he grab me by the neck or by the hair, rub up against me, or put his hand on my crotch. The fisherman Pino is no more, either, the house has been sold, everything is gone forever. My not hearing so well with my left ear might not be the result of a punch in the head but of old age; my uncle was also hard of hearing when he was around sixty, and my father never walloped him. Is my mother deaf because she's the sister of my late deaf uncle or because her husband clouted her several times? My grandma, his mother-in-law, had excellent hearing up until her death. My father respected her—he was even slightly afraid of the gray, spindly backwoods matron who once almost gouged his eyes out when she caught him drooling over some Slovenian woman near the police station. Did the old bat have such a good ear because she was out of reach of my father's big paw? Was it all quite so simple? Friends of mine around my age get on my nerves when they keep going on about their parents and blame those corpses for everything bad that happened to them in their lives. I promised myself long ago that I'd take my life into my own hands. For me, having a drunken idiot for a father and a drunken mother would never be an alibi for failure. Failure? I'm not unsuccessful. My angels are by far the hottest merchandise in the city. And we're going to expand our range even further: soon you'll be able to buy tablecloths spangled with angels, umbrellas, umbrella stands, paper napkins, flower vases, panties for angels, panties and men's boxer shorts with angels, tiny shoes and gloves for angels . . . No Croatian home should be without a guardian angel. I'm happy, happy, happy; there are few people who can stroll through Istanbul, and stop and sit down at will and dissolve granules of apple tea in hot water.

"I went to the toilet by myself today, but I didn't do a number two. The therapist wanted me to walk to the restaurant, but everything hurt, so I stayed in bed."

"She's lying, she didn't go to the toilet, and she crapped her bed. The nurses are very annoyed with her because she refuses diapers, and she doesn't go to the toilet, she always lies to you, if you don't believe me, ask one of the nurses."

While the Immobile Woman spoke I looked at my mother in the Turkish pink pajamas.

"What's she saying? Is she saying I'm bad?"

"The lady says her legs hurt, they're like two posts, the nurses turn her every two hours, day and night," I hollered.

"Has someone died?"

"Mom, why don't you put your glasses on? You've got the Novi list to read, look at the death notices yourself, get into gear a bit. I'll raise the head end of your bed, where's the remote?"

"See, you can't get it to work, Tiny knows how to adjust my bed. Cover up my legs."

90

Who is my mother today? She's an old, frail woman who says life is lovely if you can sleep. I ought to love her, be understanding, and kiss her splotchy face even if it kills me. Goodness is being able to quell your bitterness and anger.

I watched the phone. It rang, rang, and rang. I didn't answer it. I cried and shouted loudly: "I can't, I can't, I can't."

"You really overdo it," Ana said. "Your mother is just skin and bone, a benign soul who hasn't got long to go. Why so much passion?

What if you were in my position? I can't stick the old lady in a home, so I zip in to see her three times a day, I change her and spoon-feed her, and late in the evening I help my granddaughter with geography. She's only nine, but she has to know that the Dobra River is a disappearing stream, and that the oldest hydroelectric power station, Zeleni Vir, below Skrad, was built in 1921 and is still operational, and I have to know how to fold an origami frog or fish, and do you know who eats flies, beetles, and mosquitoes on Mali Lošinj Island?"

"No."

"*Tarentola mauritanica*, the common or Moorish wall gecko."

91

If my mother hadn't had children, what would her fate have been? She certainly wouldn't have stuck with my father because, in those times, men didn't stay with women who couldn't bear them children. If my mother hadn't had children she would have left my father, continued her education, and made something of her life in that system that preached the equality of the sexes. She'd have had her own apartment, she'd have inherited her mother's house by the sea, and she'd have been much healthier. If it weren't for my sister and me, she wouldn't dream at the age of eighty-five that she was being thrashed by my father and her mother, she'd only dream of her mother, and that, at least, would be only half as frustrating. She'd have sold the house by the sea for a hundred and fifty thousand euros, she'd be surrounded by caring people full of good will, who would put on a more convincing charade of love. I don't put on an act for her, I think children are allowed to be honest with their parents. She knows I don't like her, and she doesn't love me—isn't that terrible in old age? Is that in store for me as well? Which of us will die first, me or my husband? What would my life be like without him? When I'm old, helpless, spindly, and frail, will I wait for Tiny to bring walnuts to me, wherever I am? I love walnuts. How do you eat walnuts when you're almost ninety? As a cream? As a powder? As a smell?

I didn't pick up the receiver today or yesterday, and I'm not going to do it tomorrow. I'm not going to call her the day after tomorrow, I'm not going to call her for days, weeks, months, and years. No, no, no.

92

I WENT INTO the room and saw her bed empty. My heart fluttered. Today I know this was atrial fibrillation, and I take Rytmonorm and Marfarin.

"She was hollering and screaming so loudly that even people who were out walking around the home heard her," the Immobile Lady sobbed. "She's been screaming for days—day and night, you know. It's terrible, I don't deserve this."

"Why didn't you call and tell me you'd transferred her to the inpatient clinic?"

"We moved her just half an hour ago, we were going to call you when she'd settled in a bit." The head nurse smiled from ear to ear.

"I hear she was restless again. You told me not to come, that we'd been pampering her, and that she needed rest from us. That's why I haven't come for days."

The nurse looked at me, her blue eyes twinkled, and she smiled again from ear to ear. "She was restless, but now she's much, much better. We gave her something, so she's sleeping. You have to expect that she'll be mostly sleeping at the inpatient clinic."

I went up to the next floor. The inpatient clinic is one room with four beds, with a contorted something lying in each of them. One old woman with skinny arms and misshapen legs muttered, a second lay there like a corpse, the one by the window gazed at me with gray eyes—I smiled at her in vain—and my mother wheezed. A woman my age sat next to the woman lying on the bed like a dead cockroach on its back, and she spoke to this lady. The cockroach lady didn't react.

A nursing attendant came into the room in her shiny pink coat. "Come on, Granny," she said to my mother. She adjusted the bed so that it looked as if my mother was sitting. The woman tapped her on the face with her fingers. In vain.

"Don't wake her, let her sleep," I said.

"She has to eat. Come on, Granny, wake up, someone's come to see you, your daughter's here." She was holding a bowl full of a dark-green mixture.

My mother opened her eyes and looked at me.

"Can you see me, do you recognize me?" I yelled. I moved my face up to her blue lips.

"Why are you yelling?" she whispered. "Why are you always yelling?"

"Bravo," I shouted. "Bravo! Eat this and you'll feel better straight-away."

The nurse hung a napkin around her neck and spooned the mixture into her open mouth. My mother swallowed like a robot or some huge, tired, hungry bird. Then at one point she squeezed her purple lips shut.

"Almost, Granny, well done. We've eaten quite a bit. And now we'll have a nice nap." The nursing attendant lowered the backrest of the bed.

"Why is she sleeping?"

"They gave her something. What matters is that she's not in pain anymore."

The lady whose mother was the dead cockroach left the room together with me, but we didn't talk. My husband was waiting for me in the car; he didn't want to go into the inpatient clinic out of respect for the living dead, who can sometimes completely uncover themselves in their sleep. I cried.

"The nursing attendant said she's not in pain *anymore*, but otherwise they've been telling me she's not in pain *at all* . . ."

"Calm down, calm down, imagine if she had to go through all that alone, how terrible it would be, and how much she'd suffer. She has a whole team of highly qualified people around her who know best what to do and how to do it. We should be glad that we're able to pay for it all."

He stroked my knee, but I tensed up.

Oriana Fallaci wrote a book about the Vietnam War. Surrounded by mounds of young corpses, she asked how it was possible for someone back in Italy to cry over an old man who died after reaching eighty-eight. How could it be that I was getting worked up about an ancient mother who might be on her deathbed? Why was I so restless?

Ana said into the receiver: "You're anxious because you don't have any problems, babe. Do you know what the branches of sheep raising are—sorry, not sheep raising but livestock farming? Livestock farming is divided into sheep raising, poultry farming, cattle breeding, and hog raising. Crop farming is divided into vegetable growing, fruit growing, viticulture, and olive-growing. Everything else falls into fishing, forestry, hunting, and apiculture. The poor children."

I called her. Every patient had a phone on their night table in the inpatient clinic as well.

It rang and rang. No one answered. I was relieved.

93

My mother's face was yellow. She stared at me.

"How are you, do you recognize me?"

She stretched her toothless mouth.

"Bravo," I yelled.

She looked at me with one eye.

The dead cockroach muttered, one of the beds was empty, a young male nurse was changing the diaper of one of the ladies. I felt awkward. It seemed to me that changing diapers was definitively not man's work and the guy must feel terrible.

He glanced at me and smiled. "I'll change Grandma too . . . ," he said, looking at my mother, "when you go."

"You can change her while I'm here, I'm not leaving in a hurry."

My heart fluttered. If I'd known I have atrial fibrillation I might have been very concerned. It's a dangerous condition, after all. If the heart contracts like that for more than half an hour, the blood coagulates, and when the heart gets back to sinus rhythm it sends out clots in all directions, most often to the brain. I found out all that later. I stood by my mother's bed and waited. What do you call a man who changes old women's diapers? Mister? Male nurse? Murse?

He went up to my mother, uncovered her, and took off her pajama bottoms. I was appalled at how skinny she was. An ancient, premature baby in a pale-green diaper. I moved closer to the bed. He removed the wet diaper. My mother started to groan.

"Good, good, Granny, everything will be fine, just a moment longer."

He changed her diaper and looked at me. "Did you know your mother didn't pass stool yesterday either?"

I regained my breath. "How come?"

"I don't know, we'll have to give her some warm, very sweet chamomile, we definitely can't give her an enema. She needs to have regular bowel movements so it doesn't come to the worst. But I'll leave you two alone for now."

He went out of the room through the door that's never closed. If my mother had regular bowel movements, I would have found out how she smelled.

I brought my face close to hers and said loudly: "Mom, is there anything you need? I'll come again tomorrow. The main thing is that you're not in pain, you'll never be in pain again, they're giving you something, Mom . . ."

She didn't open her eyes, but she breathed calmly.

94

ANA SAID: "WHEN you're sixty, the only good mother is a dead mother."

She wasn't answering the phone, so I called the nurse.

"How's my mom?"

"She's calm and sleeping."

"Can you tell me what's happening to her?"

"What do you mean?"

"She seems somehow weak and subdued. You said she was depressive and had phantom pain, now she's totally intoxicated from the medication. Can you do anything so that she's free of pain and also conscious?"

The nurse laughed cheerfully. "You have to be patient, your mom is well and will be even better . . ."

"That inpatient clinic—isn't it for the ones who . . ."

The nurse laughed cheerfully again. "No, the inpatient clinic isn't for the terminally ill. Have you seen the lady lying in the corner?" She meant the dead cockroach. "You see, we've been supporting her for three years. So don't you worry."

"Should I come today? Does it make any sense, does she miss me?"

"Your mom is sleeping peacefully, there's no need at all for you to come, just be calm."

95

How terrible it must be for my old maid of a mother to be changed by a man. Her, of all people, who told me her whole life long that men didn't interest her and that they'd be my ruin. And now a kid who could be her grandson spreads her legs; he prattles to her, strokes her face, and combs her gray fuzz. I ought to be satisfied. This is my mother's punishment. Finally, now, on her deathbed, she's paying for all the evil she did to me: for the drunken nights, for the staring into space, for the looking through me while I screamed when my father beat me, for all the reluctant breastfeeding . . . God is now meting out his punishment, although she never believed in God; she's paying a terrible price for her crimes, I ought to be happy. I should be relaxed. I really shouldn't look at the fridge and cry when I see my chosen grandma, my little old granny from Belgrade, and Ana. Why am I crying? I'm a pathos-ridden old lady full of self-pity. I ought to call Ana, she'd tell me what real problems are. Her granddaughter has scarlet fever, her son has lost his job, her mother has diarrhea and needs her diaper changed nine times a day, nine times five kuna—have fun dealing with all that! Still, Ana produces those angels at night. You don't see at work how many problems she has.

Why can't my old mother be a test of my mettle? I'm no good, but I ought to prove to her that I'm better than her, warmer, more patient and tender . . . I'm not. I can't put it on. I don't want to. I can't forgive her. When I was small and my father belted me . . . When I was a girl and my father slavered over me . . . Again and again. For how long? My stinking father. Stinking father? I ask myself every day, although it's not fair, how much our fathers would have stunk if our mothers hadn't been sitting nearby. Our helpless, dallying, quiet, gaunt, disheveled, intimidated, euthanized mothers. If my mother had killed my father I'd be a better person. Instead, she sent me a message as if to say: Fuck you, I'm looking after number one, I'm keeping my peace of mind in my bottle of rum. Can we really always be on our mothers' side after all they never did for us? How do our mothers smell, how does my mom smell?

Who is lying in that bed? My mother?

That is my mother?!

96

AND WHAT KIND of mom am I? I can't stand alcohol. Tiny's father is a magnificent man who brings me a decaf macchiato from his bar whenever I'm in the shop. I don't embrace or kiss my daughter, or, to be more exact, I never take the first step; but whenever she sees me, she comes up and hugs me and kisses me on the cheek, or offers me hers for a kiss. I don't hate my daughter, I don't snarl at her, I buy her jewelry and jackets, I'm always telling her she's a gorgeous young woman, both pretty and intelligent, and we're in touch at least three times a day. No, I'm not like my mother, I'm not my mom. Our daughter didn't interfere with my trajectory, she didn't spoil a single one of my plans, I didn't breastfeed her against my will, in fact I didn't breastfeed her at all because she was born at a time when breastfeeding wasn't in fashion. Milk formulas were advertised on TV the way cell phones are today, and we seventies moms were more afraid of sagging breasts than cancer. I'm not my mom, so I really have no idea how I smell to my daughter. Does she sniff me when she hugs and kisses me? I'm not my mom, I'm really not, I'm not a depressive old bitch who bites her daughter. Unlike her, I have grasped life by the horns, and I'm still holding those horns in my hands. Will my daughter never, never, never leave the room when a nursing attendant comes to change my diapers?

97

The phone rang. Six in the morning. Saturday. I put on my glasses and glanced at the display. The home.

"Your mother developed a high temperature during the night. A hundred and seven. We're getting her ready just now."

I was horrified. "A hundred and seven, what could that be? Perhaps she's got pneumonia . . ."

"Perhaps."

"What do you think, is there any point in me going to the hospital and waiting for her there?"

"No, she's not well, you'd only unsettle her. They have to do tests and scans, then they'll send her back. Come in the afternoon."

Death? Was this death? It could only be death, right? Who can survive pneumonia at the age of eighty-four? What if she died in the hospital alone, without anyone else around?

"We're going," I told my husband.

"No we're not. Why should we?" my husband said. "Either she'll pull through or she'll die, you can't do anything about it, she'd just get terribly upset."

"I don't want my mother to die like a dog in some broom closet, I watched her mother dying like that."

"That was a hundred years ago, and hospitals don't have broom closets anymore, every little room is put to use, people die in company these days, separated from one another by partitions. Your mom won't die alone."

I looked through the window at the begonia, the only sort that tolerates bright sun. It's called Dragon Wing. Dark red. If my mother dies, if this is the end, we'll heave a sigh of relief when I just remember that she never loved me, and that I paid a thousandfold for her milk that I drank. Besides, I'm already old, what do I need a mom for, why would I need that spiteful old relic, that malicious mother screaming in phantom pain and finding fault with everything, the tea has to be iced tea and peach flavored, she can only drink the coffee from the vending machine if Tiny gets it for her, I don't know how to adjust the bed or cover her up properly. I got up, opened her old satchel, and found a picture in it of her smiling in the brightly colored dress my father once bought for her. She wore it for years, for decades. The woman looking at me from the small photo was much younger than I am today, but uncared for. Disheveled gray hair, but in a careless, cheerfully untidy sort of way. My mom's eyes shone—who knows why she was smiling. If my mom had stayed that woman, could I have loved her?

98

"Your mom is back but she's not well. Come this way, please."

She was lying alone in a small room. The male nurse was taking her temperature. "Ninety-five point four."

"Why is that?"

He uncovered my mother's legs and pointed to her swollen ankles.

"That's it."

"What's what?"

"You have to be brave now, I think she's going, she's leaving us." He patted me on the shoulder.

"Mom," I shouted and held my face up to hers, "Mom!"

She breathed quietly.

"Mom, do you recognize me? Mom!"

Her mouth was half open, her eyes shut. I sniffed and nuzzled around her until my face was almost sticking together with hers. I went out.

The head nurse looked at me and didn't smile from ear to ear.

"It's incredible, her lab results are a disaster," she said. "They X-rayed her lungs and discovered metastases on the bones, she must have suffered terribly all this time . . ."

I looked her in the eyes.

99

Yesterday we placed her urn in the common grave because the niche for it isn't ready yet. We chose a wonderful niche with a view of the sea, and my mom and I will rest there as dust together.

I sit in our living room, the birds fly low, there will be rain. My mom watches me from that photograph, she smiles at me and her eyes shine, and the brightly colored dress is so cheery. I get up and stick my mom to the fridge door, held there by Chagall's *Laiterie*: a large cow's head, a big, dark-brown eye, and on the cow's head a woman milking a blue cow.

100

Tiny comes into the room. She hugs and kisses me. I push her off a little.

"Tell me, what do I smell like?"

My daughter looks at me with her sparkling brown eyes: "Coco Mademoiselle."

Selected Dalkey Archive Paperbacks

Michal Ajvaz, *Empty Streets*
Journey to the South
The Golden Age
The Other City
David Albahari, *Gotz & Meyer*
Learning Cyrillic
Pierre Albert-Birot, *The First Book of Grabinoulor*
Svetlana Alexievich, *Voices from Chernobyl*
Felipe Alfau, *Chromos*
Locos
João Almino, *Enigmas of Spring*
Free City
The Book of Emotions
Ivan Ângelo, *The Celebration*
David Antin, *Talking*
Djuna Barnes, *Ladies Almanack*
Ryder
John Barth, *The End of the Road*
The Floating Opera
The Tidewater Tales
Donald Barthelme, *Paradise*
The King
Svetislav Basara, *Chinese Letter*
Fata Morgana
The Mongolian Travel Guide
Andrej Blatnik, *Law of Desire*
You Do Understand
Patrick Bolshauser, *Rapids*
Louis Paul Boon, *Chapel Road*
My Little War
Summer in Termuren
Roger Boylan, *Killoyle*
Ignacio de Loyola Brandão, *And Still the Earth*
Anonymous Celebrity
The Good-Bye Angel
Sébastien Brebel, *Francis Bacon's Armchair*
Christine Brooke-Rose, *Amalgamemnon*
Brigid Brophy, *In Transit*
Prancing Novelist: In Praise of Ronald Firbank
Gerald L. Bruns, *Modern Poetry and the Idea of Language*
Lasha Bugadze, *The Literature Express*
Dror Burstein, *Kin*
Michel Butor, *Mobile*
Julieta Campos, *The Fear of Losing Eurydice*
Anne Carson, *Eros the Bittersweet*
Camilo José Cela, *Family of Pascual Duarte*
Louis-Ferdinand Céline, *Castle to Castle*
Hugo Charteris, *The Tide Is Right*
Luis Chitarroni, *The No Variations*
Jack Cox, *Dodge Rose*
Ralph Cusack, *Cadenza*
Stanley Crawford, *Log of the S.S. the Mrs. Unguentine*
Some Instructions to My Wife
Robert Creeley, *Collected Prose*
Nicholas Delbanco, *Sherbrookes*
Rikki Ducornet, *The Complete Butcher's Tales*
William Eastlake, *Castle Keep*
Stanley Elkin, *The Dick Gibson Show*
The Magic Kingdom
Gustave Flaubert, *Bouvard et Pécuchet*
Jon Fosse, *Melancholy I*
Melancholy II
Trilogy
Max Frisch, *I'm Not Stiller*
Man in the Holocene
Carlos Fuentes, *Christopher Unborn*
Great Latin American Novel
Nietzsche on His Balcony
Terra Nostra
Where the Air Is Clear
William Gaddis, *J R*
The Recognitions
William H. Gass, *A Temple of Texts*
Cartesian Sonata and Other Novellas
Finding a Form
Life Sentences
Reading Rilke
Tests of Time: Essays
The Tunnel
Willie Masters' Lonesome Wife
World Within the Word
Etienne Gilson, *Forms and Substances in the Arts*
The Arts of the Beautiful
Douglas Glover, *Bad News of the Heart*
Paulo Emílio Sales Gomes, *P's Three Women*
Juan Goytisolo, *Count Julian*
Juan the Landless
Marks of Identity
Alasdair Gray, *Poor Things*
Jack Green, *Fire the Bastards!*
Jiří Gruša, *The Questionnaire*
Mela Hartwig, *Am I a Redundant Human Being?*
John Hawkes, *The Passion Artist*
Dermot Healy, *Fighting with Shadows*
The Collected Short Stories
Aidan Higgins, *A Bestiary*
Bornholm Night-Ferry
Langrishe, Go Down
Scenes from a Receding Past
Aldous Huxley, *Point Counter Point*
Those Barren Leaves
Time Must Have a Stop
Drago Jančar, *The Galley Slave*
I Saw Her That Night
The Tree with No Name
Gert Jonke, *Awakening to the Great Sleep War*
Geometric Regional Novel
Homage to Czerny
The Distant Sound
The System of Vienna
Guillermo Cabrera Infante, *Infante's Inferno*
Three Trapped Tigers
Jacques Jouet, *Mountain R*
Mieko Kanai, *The Word Book*
Yorum Kaniuk, *Life on Sandpaper*
Ignacy Karpowicz, *Gestures*
Pablo Katchadjian, *What to Do*
Hugh Kenner, *The Counterfeiters*
Flaubert, Joyce, and Beckett: The Stoic Comedians
Gnomon
Joyce's Voices
Danilo Kiš, *A Tomb for Boris Davidovich*
Garden, Ashes
Pierre Klossowski, *Roberte Ce Soir and The Revocation of the Edict of Nantes*
George Konrád, *The City Builder*
Tadeusz Konwicki, *The Polish Complex*
Elaine Kraf, *The Princess of 72nd Street*
Édouard Levé, *Suicide*
Mario Levi, *Istanbul Was a Fairytale*
Deborah Levy, *Billy & Girl*
José Lezama Lima, *Paradiso*
Osman Lins, *Avalovara*
António Lobo Antunes, *Knowledge of Hell*
The Splendor of Portugal
Mina Loy, *Stories and Essays of Mina Loy*
Joaquim Maria Machado de Assis, *Collected Stories*
Alf Maclochlainn, *Out of Focus*
Ford Madox Ford, *The March of Literature*
D. Keith Mano, *Take Five*
Micheline Marcom, *A Brief History of Yes*
The Mirror in the Well
Ben Marcus, *The Age of Wire and String*
Wallace Markfield, *Teitlebaum's Widow*
To an Early Grave
David Markson, *Reader's Block*
Wittgenstein's Mistress
Carole Maso, *AVA*

Harry Mathews, *My Life in CIA*
Singular Pleasures
The Case of the Persevering Maltese: Collected Essays
Herman Melville, *The Confidence-Man: His Masquerade*
Steven Milhauser, *In the Penny Arcade*
The Barnum Museum
Christine Montalbetti, *American Journal*
The Origin of Man
Western
Nicholas Mosley, *Accident*
Experience and Religion
Hopeful Monsters
Imago Bird
Impossible Object
Judith
Metamorphosis
Natalie Natalia
Serpent
The Uses of Slime Mould: Essays of Four Decades
Time at War
Warren Motte, *OULIPO: A Primer of Potential Literature*
Gerald Murnane, *Barley Patch*
Inland
Mihkel Mutt, *The Inner Immigrant*
Yves Navarre, *Our Share of Time*
Dorothy Nelson, *In Night's City*
Tar and Feathers
Boris A. Novak, *The Master of Insomnia: Selected Poems*
Flann O'Brien, *At Swim-Two-Birds*
At War
Further Cuttings from Cruiskeen Lawn
Plays and Teleplays
The Best of Myles
The Collected Letters
The Dalkey Archive
The Hard Life
The Poor Mouth
The Short Fiction of Flann O'Brien
The Third Policeman
Máirtín Ó Cadhain, *The Key/An Eochair*
Patrik Ouředník, *Case Closed*
Europeana: A Brief History of the Twentieth Century
The Opportune Moment, 1855
Arvo Pärt, *Arvo Pärt in Conversation*
Robert Pinget, *The Inquisitory*
Raymond Queneau, *Odile*
Pierrot Mon Ami
Ann Quin, *Berg*
Passages
Tripticks
Ishmael Reed, *Juice!*
Reckless Eyeballing
The Free-Lance Pallbearers
The Last Days of Louisiana Red
The Terrible Threes
The Terrible Twos
Yellow Back Radio Broke-Down
Noëlle Revaz, *With the Animals*
Rainer Maria Rilke, *The Notebooks of Malte Laurids Brigge*
Julián Ríos, *Larva: Midsummer Night's Babel*
Augusto Roa Bastos, *I the Supreme*
Alain Robbe-Grillet, *Project for a Revolution in New York*
Daniël Robberechts, *Arriving in Avignon*
Writing Prague
Olivier Rolin, *Hotel Crystal*
Jacques Roubaud, *Mathematics*
Some Thing Black
The Great Fire of London
The Plurality of Worlds of Lewis
Vedrana Rudan, *Love at Last Sight*
Night
Stig Sæterbakken, *Don't Leave Me*
Invisible Hands
Self-Control
Siamese
Through the Night
Lydie Salvayre, *The Company of Ghosts*
Severo Sarduy, *Cobra & Maitreya*
Nathalie Sarraute, *Do You Hear Them?*
Martereau
The Planetarium
Arno Schmidt, *Collected Novellas*
Collected Stories
Nobodaddy's Children
Two Novels
Asaf Schurr, *Motti*
Pierre Senges, *Fragments of Lichtenberg*
Elizabeth Sewell, *The Field of Nonsense*
Bernard Share, *Transit*
Youval Shimoni, *A Room*
Viktor Shklovsky, *A Hunt for Optimism*
A Sentimental Journey: Memoirs 1917-1922
Bowstring
Energy of Delusion: A Book on Plot
Knight's Move
Life of a Bishop's Assistant
Literature and Cinematography
The Hamburg Score
Theory of Prose
Third Factory
Zoo, or Letters Not About Love
Kjesrsti Skomsvold, *Monsterhuman*
The Faster I Walk, the Smaller I Am
Josef Skvorecky, *The Engineer of Human Souls*
Gilbert Sorrentino, *Aberration of Starlight*
Crystal Vision
Imaginative Qualities of Actual Things
Mulligan Stew
Pack of Lies: A Trilogy
Splendide-Hôtel
The Sky Changes
Gertrude Stein, *A Novel of Thank You*
Lucy Church Amiably
The Making of Americans
Gonçalo M. Tavares, *Jerusalem*
Joseph Walser's Machine
Lygia Fagundes Telles, *The Girl in the Photograph*
Nikanor Tetralogen, *Assisted Living*
Stefan Themerson, *Hobson's Island*
Tom Harris
John Toomey, *Huddleston Road*
Sleepwalker
Slipping
Jáchym Topol, *Angel Station*
Jean-Philippe Toussaint, *Monsieur*
Running Away
Television
The Bathroom
Dumitru Tsepeneag, *Hotel Europa*
La Belle Roumaine
Pigeon Post
The Bulgarian Truck
The Necessary Marriage
Vain Art of the Fugue
Waiting
Dubravka Ugresic, *Lend Me Your Character*
Thank You for Not Reading
Tor Ulven, *Replacement*
Mati Unt, *Things in the Night*
Paul Verhaeghen, *Omega Minor*
Boris Vian, *Heartsnatcher*
Nick Wadley, *Man + Dog*
Man + Table
Markus Werner, *Cold Shoulder*
Zündel's Exit
Curtis White, *Memories of My Father Watching TV*
Douglas Woolf, *Wall to Wall*
Philip Wylie, *Generation of Vipers*
Marguerite Young, *Miss Macintosh My Darling*
Louis Zukofsky, *Collected Fiction*